DISCARD

less than perfect

BY LOUISE ALBERT

HOLIDAY HOUSE / NEW YORK

The poem "Filling Corners, Filling Moments," was originally published in the poetry collection *While The Music Is Playing* by Floyd Albert (Lewiston, NY: Mellen Poetry Press, an imprint of The Edwin Mellen Press, 2002). The poem is reprinted on pages 36–37 by permission of Mellen Poetry Press.

The poem "Laura the Lion," is reprinted on page 167 by permission of Floyd Albert.

1 3 5 7 9 10 8 6 4 2

Library of Congress Cataloging-in-Publication Data
Albert, Louise.
Less Than Perfect / by Louise Albert.
p.   cm.
Summary: Fifteen-year-old Laura finds her life terribly complicated
when she meets an interesting boy and her mother is diagnosed with breast cancer.
ISBN 0-8234-1688-7 (hardcover)
[1. Cancer—Fiction. 2. Mothers and daughters—Fiction.]
PZ7.A3213 Les 2003
[Fic]—dc21   2001039303

For
Floyd
And
Suzanne Reinoehl

A special thanks to Marilyn Seymour, Arlene Edelson,
Ellen Schmidt, and Bernice Wilson for their encouragement
and for reading the manuscript in its many stages.

chapter one

Laura was lying.

"Are you sure you won't come with us?" her mother asked. "Charlie's going to be disappointed."

"I know, but I'll see him tonight."

She'd told her parents at breakfast that she wanted to stay home. They were going to pick up her brother at his music camp in the Berkshires. He and several other advanced kids had stayed on for an extra week of special instruction. Laura had said she needed to start reading *A Tale of Two Cities*, the first book on her reading list for her sophomore year.

She almost never lied to her mother, but she couldn't bear driving back with Charlie. Her parents would go on and on about the prize he had won for his piano playing, and how his counselors said he had so much talent, and how they expected great things from him in the future. Besides, spending two hours in the car with her mother wasn't something she wanted to do, either. Lately, Laura tried to avoid her whenever she could, because one minute her mother

1

would make a big fuss about nothing, and the next minute she would be all lovey-dovey.

Her father was already backing the car out of their garage as Laura walked out to the porch with her mother.

"I wish I were fifteen again and spending a relaxing day sunbathing and reading *A Tale of Two Cities*," her mother said. "I don't have that kind of free time anymore." She sighed. "It's wonderful to be young."

Her mother handed Laura a bottle of sunscreen. "Promise me you'll wear this today. Blondes have to be especially careful."

"I'll put it on later," Laura said. "I want to get a base tan first."

"Excuse me," her mother said. "I don't think so. Put some on now." She folded her arms and waited. "I'm not leaving until I see you put it on."

"Mom!" Laura cried. "I've been out on the deck a thousand times without sunblock."

"Not anymore," her mother said.

Laura frowned but rubbed some lotion on her face. "I'll put more on after I change clothes."

Her mother's face softened. "Thank you. I know you will. It's just so important."

"Annie, come on!" her father called from the car.

"Okay, okay, I'm coming." But instead of going down the porch steps, she gently pushed Laura's hair behind her ears and gave her a hug.

Laura laughed. "Mom, you're only going to be gone for the day."

"I know. I love you, sweetie," she said, and hugged Laura again. Then she stepped back and took a long look at Laura. She was smiling, but Laura thought she caught the glimmer of tears in her mother's eyes, too. Laura suddenly shivered, even in the warmth of the sun.

"Mom—" she started.

"See you later, sweetie," her mother interrupted, and hurried down the porch steps.

The car backed down the driveway and turned into the road. Laura stared after it until the chill inside her finally disappeared.

In the bedroom Laura took off her pajamas and looked in the mirror over her dresser. She could see herself only from the waist up. She remembered seeing her mother looking at herself in the mirror the same way the day before. On her way to the bathroom, Laura had glanced into her parents' room. The door was partly open and her mother was looking in the mirror at her naked body, studying herself.

Laura turned her body to a profile and then back to a full view. A few years ago Laura had wondered if she'd ever need to wear a bra. Now she knew she didn't have to worry about that anymore.

She put on a pair of really short shorts and a halter top, hoping she could get a darker tan before she went back to school. Then she rubbed in a light coat of sunscreen.

Stretched out on a lounge chair on the deck behind the house, she opened the book and started to read. She was just beginning the third chapter when a large blond dog ran onto the lawn beyond the deck, his leash trailing from his collar.

"Folly! Folly!" a boy was calling and running after the dog. Finally the dog lay down on the grass, and the boy grabbed the leash. He had light brown hair and looked about her age. He was a bit short, but Laura liked his face.

"Sorry," he said to Laura. Then he turned to the dog. "Listen, fella, don't do that again or you'll be in big trouble."

"What kind of trouble?" Laura asked, getting up. "I hope you don't believe in capital punishment for dogs."

"No, I don't. But I know they have a leash law around here, so if I get a ticket, I'll tell them it was Folly's fault and they should put him in jail and only give him bread and water."

The dog stood on his hind legs, wagged his tail, and tried to lick the boy's face.

"He's really afraid of you," Laura said, and laughed.

"Yeah. What can I do? He loves me. And I thought I could trust him. I let go of the leash for just a second so I could tie my laces—and he ran off."

Laura looked down at his sneakers.

"I know—they're still untied. I figured I'd better catch him before he ran too far away and got lost—or run over. But I almost broke my neck with these things so loose."

He knelt down, and still holding the leash, he tried again to tie his laces. It seemed too complicated, so he put the leash under one of his feet and started tying the other one.

The dog gave a big tug, pulled the leash free, and ran back to the street.

"Oh no!" the boy groaned, and then shouted, "Folly, come back here, you dumb dog."

The dog was out of sight.

"See you," the boy called to Laura, and then he was gone.

Laura went back to her book, but now it was hard to concentrate. She wondered where the boy lived. Probably somewhere in the neighborhood, she thought, though she had never seen him before. Maybe he had just moved here. She'd look for him when school started.

chapter two

Charlie and her mother were talking downstairs in the kitchen. It was almost eight fifteen. Usually they were both finished with their breakfast by now and Laura had the kitchen to herself. School had started a few days ago with new classes, new teachers, and her friends from last year scattered all over the large building. Every morning she woke up excited but also with a knot of anxiety in her stomach. The last thing she wanted when she went downstairs were questions, advice, or arguments. Well, if she waited any longer, she'd be late.

Her mother was loading the dishwasher. Charlie, finishing a dish of scrambled eggs, looked up at her through glasses, which, as usual, needed cleaning. His brown hair fell across his forehead, almost touching his eyes.

Laura put her books down on the table and poured herself a glass of orange juice.

"I gotta go. I'm meeting Michael." Charlie got up from the table with a piece of toast in his hand. "Hi, Laura. Bye, Laura," he said, and tapped her lightly on the head. Even though he was only thirteen, they were about the same height.

"Thanks, pal," she said, tapping him back. "And in case you're interested, your glasses are a mess."

"Things look better this way." He finished his toast and rushed out the door.

"What kind of eggs do you want?" her mother asked.

"No eggs today, Mom. I'm not hungry."

"I hate to see you go to school on an empty stomach."

"I'll be fine," Laura said. "I have an early lunch period— which reminds me. My lunch money's upstairs." As she left the kitchen she passed her father coming in with his briefcase.

Halfway up the stairs, she heard her father whisper, "I'll meet you there at eleven." Laura stood still. Her mother was supposed to be teaching at the college this morning.

"Okay," her mother said.

"Don't worry, babe," her father said. "It's going to be all right." Then she heard him go out the kitchen door.

After grabbing her wallet off her desk, Laura gathered up her books from the kitchen. Her mother was at the table drinking coffee, *The New York Times* spread open before her. Laura was half out the door when her mother called to her, "Don't say good-bye, whatever you do."

Laura stopped. "Sorry," she said. Her mother's head stayed bent over the paper. "Are you okay, Mom?"

"Yes. I'm okay," she said. But she didn't look okay.

"I'm sorry I didn't say good-bye," Laura said, and then with a big smile, she called out, "Good-bye, good-bye, good-bye."

Her mother didn't smile back. "You'd better go, or you'll be late."

A few moments later, wheeling her bike past the kitchen window, Laura saw her mother put her hands over her face. She stopped. Maybe she should go back. Then her mother got up and left the kitchen. Laura hesitated, then rode down the hill toward school.

The cool air rushing past her felt good, but it was hard to stop wondering what her mother was so upset about. Maybe her father was losing his job. He was a lawyer in a big firm in New York. He mostly handled public service cases, often defending people who were sentenced to death. Laura thought they must be interesting cases, but her father rarely spoke about his work. He was such a quiet man, it was hard to get him to talk. It was her mother who told Laura and Charlie that business wasn't so good these days at the firm and that someone in their father's office had just been let go. But they wouldn't do that to her father. He was so smart and he worked so hard.

Laura turned left and started down Ridgeview. Toward the end of the street a boy was walking his dog. When she rode closer, she saw it was the same dog and same boy from a few days ago. She slowed down and got off her bike.

"Hey," the boy said. "I think we know each other."

"I'm not sure about you, but I know your bad, bad dog."

"Uh-oh. Does that mean I'm so forgettable?"

"Well . . ." She laughed.

Folly came over to her with his tail wagging.

"What kind of dog is he?" she asked, petting him.

"A golden retriever. I think you've made a friend."

The boy looked at his watch. "I'd better go or I'll be late." He tugged on Folly's leash and they were off down the road—away from Laura's school.

*   *   *

At lunchtime, Laura looked around the cafeteria, but there was no sign of the boy. Carrying her tray, she found an empty table and saw her friend Rachel heading toward her.

"Sorry I'm late," Rachel said. She was tall and thin like Laura, and they both had long hair, but Rachel's was dark and wavy. "I was getting my English paper back."

"I'll forgive you this time. But only because I was afraid I was going to have to eat alone." Laura smiled. "Everyone else I know has lunch next period. So how'd you do on that in-class paper? I can't believe she gave it to us the first week of school. I got an A minus."

Laura and Rachel were both in an honors English class, but in different sections. Laura had gotten her paper back earlier that morning.

"I did all right," Rachel said. "Mrs. Forrest is a tough grader, though." She took a paper sack out of her book bag. Laura knew what was likely to be inside. Rachel's favorite lunch was a concoction of yogurt, cut-up fruit, and nuts, and wheat germ in a plastic container.

"I'm going to get some milk," Rachel said. "Want anything?"

"No, thanks."

Laura saw Rachel's paper sticking out of a spiral notebook in her book bag. She glanced across the room. Rachel was in a long line to pay for her milk, so Laura pulled the paper up a couple of inches and saw Mrs. Forrest's handwriting on the top of the page. "A+—a fine job, Rachel. Full of wonderful ideas. A pleasure to read." Rachel had done more than just all right.

Laura quickly pushed the paper back into the notebook and started eating her hamburger. In a few minutes Rachel returned with a small carton of skim milk.

She took the lid off her plastic container and started to stir the contents with a spoon. "So, have you seen any new students? Maybe they'll be some cute new guys at our school this year."

"I have seen a cute new guy lately," Laura said. "But not here at school."

"Oooh, tell me all the details," Rachel said. "Who is the mystery man? And where does he go to school?"

"I don't know his name, but I know he has a dog," Laura said.

Rachel rolled her eyes. "You'd never make it as a detective."

"The dog's name is Folly," Laura tried again.

"Well, that's a start," said Rachel. "Maybe Folly will be listed in the phone book."

They both broke into laughter.

Biking home that afternoon, Laura saw the big golden retriever again. But this time a rather plump woman with short dark hair was holding his leash. Laura stopped her bike and got off.

"That's a beautiful dog," she said.

"Oh, thank you. Yes, he is. Aren't you, Folly, old thing." The woman patted the dog's smooth blond back.

"How'd he get a name like that?"

"Well, he's Paul's Folly. Folly for short. Paul's my son, and we told him that it would be absolute folly to get a dog that would grow so big—we lived in an apartment in the city then—but he was the most adorable puppy, and none of us could resist him." She smiled at Laura.

"Well, I wish I had a folly like that," Laura said. "But my mother's allergic, so we don't even have a cat."

"That's too bad. But I envy you your bike. I used to love bike riding. Yours looks very sporty. What kind is it?"

"A Bianchi mountain bike," Laura said. "It has twenty-one speeds. I had to save for two years to buy it."

"Well, it looks like it was worth it. Leave it to the Italians. They know how to do everything right—food, wine, opera—even bikes." She grinned at Laura.

Laura swung her leg back over her bike. The dog came over and sniffed at her.

"Come on, Folly," the woman said. "I know you wish you could go home with her instead of dragging around with an old lady like me, but you can't." She pulled him away. "Anyway, we've got to get home."

Maybe Paul didn't live in Edgemont, where Laura lived, but a few blocks away in Hartsdale and he went to Woodlands. That would explain why she didn't see him at school.

Laura put one foot inside the stirrup. "Well, I'd better go, too," she said, and rode toward home.

chapter three

Laura sat in a small cubicle in the public library. It was Tuesday, and she had to write a paper on *A Tale of Two Cities*. Mrs. Forrest gave them several topics to choose from, but she wanted them to use the library for their research. She said too many students had forgotten how to use the library because they used the Internet so much.

After two hours of research Laura decided she had done enough. She stood up to put her things together and heard someone say, "Hi."

In the cubicle on the other side of hers, looking up and smiling at her, was Paul.

"Oh, hi," Laura said. "I almost didn't recognize you without your dog."

"I almost didn't recognize you without your bike." He stood up and stuffed his books into his backpack.

"This place is too quiet," he said as they walked through the library toward the front doors. "I can't concentrate. They should change their signs to say 'Noise, please.' Then I'd feel like I was in my room with my stereo on."

She smiled at him. His eyes were a soft brown, with a kind of liveliness to them.

"Maybe they should have a special room," she said. "With a stereo going full blast, and a tape of someone's mother yelling that you should turn it down or you'll go deaf, and why aren't you cleaning up your room."

"I'll volunteer my mom for the part," he said.

"So, Paul, how's Folly?" She was pleased by his look of surprise.

"Hey, how'd you know my name?"

"ESP. I'm psychic."

"You must be. What else do you know? You've got me worried."

They were outside now and walking toward the bike rack.

"You should be worried," she said with a grin.

"Uh-oh. I hope you don't go blasting a guy's secrets all over the place.'

"Don't worry," she said. "I know how to keep quiet."

"Well, that's a relief. Listen, I don't have ESP. So what's your name?"

"Laura. Laura Gould," she said.

"Well, Laura Gould, what time is it?"

Laura looked at her watch. "It's almost four thirty."

"My friend's picking me up in a few minutes," he said. "Do you need a ride?"

"No, I've got my bike. But thanks for the offer. Maybe another time." She hoped he would ask her where she lived, but he didn't. "Well, see you," she said. She got on her bike and rode down the library driveway.

"See you," he called after her.

12

Laura was having a glass of milk and some Oreos when the phone rang. She answered it, but the call was for Charlie.

She was being stupid. She had been back from the library just a short time. Paul probably wasn't even home yet. Even if he were, he wasn't going to be calling her. He didn't know where she lived, and since there were several Goulds in the local phone book, he wouldn't know which Gould she was.

When the phone rang again she ran to answer it. This time her mother had picked up the phone in her bedroom, and Laura heard her say, "Hello."

"Mrs. Gould?" a man's voice asked. "This is Dr. Amurati."

"I have it, Laura," her mother said. "Please hang up."

Laura hung up the phone and headed up the stairs to start her math homework. Soon there was a knock on her door. "Come in," Laura called.

"Hi," her mother said, and smiled broadly. "How's it going?"

"How's what going?"

"I don't know. School . . ."

"It's okay," Laura replied. "But I've got a ton of home-work tonight."

"Well, I guess I should leave you to it. I'll start dinner," her mother said, still smiling. This was the happiest Laura had seen her all week. And then she leaned over and kissed Laura on the cheek. Before Laura could say anything, she had left the room.

Her mother was serving each of them a thick slice of pot roast when her father got up from the table. He opened the freezer and took out a bottle of champagne.

"Wow!" Charlie said. "Champagne! Is this *Lifestyles of the Wanna-Be-Rich-and-Famous?*"

"Champagne in the freezer?" Laura asked. "Couldn't it explode in there?"

"I just put it there a little while ago," her father said. "I bought it on my way home because we have something to celebrate."

"You won the lottery," Charlie said. "And now we really are rich, right?"

"No," her mother said. "Believe it or not, it's something better than that."

"What is it, Mom?" Laura said. "Tell us."

"Okay." Her mother took a deep breath, and her face grew more serious. "Two weeks ago my doctor found a lump in my breast, and I was afraid I had cancer."

Laura's heart seemed to stop and her hands flew up to her breasts before she knew what she was doing. Her face flushed hot with embarrassment before she quickly dropped her hands back in her lap.

"He sent me to a top-notch breast surgeon, who decided I should have a mammogram. I had one. But then yesterday," her mother continued, "I had a sonogram too because it tells you more. It looked good, but the doctor wanted a second opinion. Today he called to say that everything was fine. It was just a cyst. There was nothing to worry about. That's better than winning the lottery."

"It sure is," Laura's father said.

He twisted the wire off the top of the champagne bottle. *Bang!* The cork flew out.

"Quick, Annie, give me your glass," her father said as champagne foam began to pour onto his fingers.

Her mother held her glass to the bottle. She was smiling and giggling, almost like a kid, Laura thought. Most of all, she looked relieved.

Laura's father filled all their glasses, giving Laura and Charlie just a bit, then raised his own.

"Here's to Mom. Precious and strong. To her good health, for years and years."

Laura sipped her champagne, enjoying the sweet-dry taste and the fizzle that tickled her nose.

So this was why her mother had been acting so strangely.

"Now, I ask you," her mother said as she gave herself another slice of meat, "isn't this the most fantastic pot roast you've ever eaten?"

"Mom!" Charlie said. "You're the cook. You're not supposed to say that."

"Why not?" her mother said. "If I don't praise my cooking, who will?"

"Me," her father said. "Who else?"

"Oh, sure, Dad," Laura said, and they all laughed. Not only was her father not much of a talker, he rarely gave compliments.

"You said a mouthful!" her mother said, and then giggled. "And this is certainly the most fantastic champagne I've ever drank. Drunk? Which is it? I can never remember." She poured herself another glass. "We should have champagne more often."

"Easy does it, Annie," her father said. "You're going to be feeling this pretty soon."

"That's what I want," she said, and drained her glass. "I want to feel something, and the sooner the better. All those days of waiting—I've been numb." She reached for the bottle again. "You have some more, too, Dan." She began to pour him some champagne, but he put his hand over his glass. The champagne ran over his hand and onto the tablecloth.

"Mom!" Charlie said. "What're you doing?"

15

"I'm celebrating," his mother said. "I want Dad to celebrate with me." She picked up her glass, and seeing that it was empty, she set it down. Then she put her hands to her face and she was crying.

Laura's father leaned over and put his arm around her.

"I'm sorry." Her mother wiped her eyes with her napkin. "It's been a long day. I think I'll go lie down awhile." She got up and left the kitchen.

They finished the rest of their meal quietly.

After dinner Laura helped her father clear off the table and load the dishwasher.

"Dad," Laura said as she folded the tablecloth. "Is everything really all right?"

Her father was staring out the kitchen window into the darkness. He blinked and shook his head. "What?"

"It was good news today, right?"

Her father just turned back to the window. "Your mom's just tired. That's all." He gave a tight smile. "I'll finish up. You probably have a lot of homework."

Laura could see that her father wasn't going to say anything more about it. Maybe everything wasn't really all right. If there was something else—something that would make her mother cry—maybe her mother would tell her.

Laura went upstairs and knocked on her mother's bedroom door.

"Come in," her mother called. She was lying on her bed, reading a magazine.

"Hi," Laura said. "Want some company?"

"Sure. Come sit down. I'm sorry I fell apart at dinner."

"That's okay," Laura said. She sat down on the big chair next to the bed. "Why didn't you tell me and Charlie before, Mom?"

"I didn't want to worry you if it turned out to be unnecessary. Besides, it was hard to talk about it—even to Dad. I knew he was scared, too—but in a different way. I think it was the idea that I might have cancer—that I might die—"

Laura caught her breath.

"—but all I could think about was losing my breast," her mother continued, her eyes filling with tears. "The doctor said I was jumping to conclusions—that if the lump turned out to be malignant, almost all women have lumpectomies now. That's where they just remove the tumor. But I could only think about the worst."

Laura wanted to put her arms around her mother, but hesitated. "Oh, Mom," she said. "That must have been so awful for you."

Her mother nodded.

"Listen," Laura said, "maybe I should go and let you rest."

"No, don't go. I'm glad you're here. It feels good to be able to talk about it."

"Did you find the lump yourself?" Laura asked.

"No. Some people say you should examine your breasts regularly, and I do every once in a while, but they always seem lumpy to me, and that scares me. So I just let my gynecologist do it. I'm always so relieved when he tells me everything is normal. But this time he didn't."

"Could you feel it?"

"I could when he showed me where it was, but it was pretty small—about the size of a pea. Anyway, he said it was probably just a cyst, but that I'd better have a surgeon look at it. But you know how it is in August—so many doctors are away, so I had to wait over a week for an appointment. I think it was the longest week of my life."

"I can imagine," Laura said. She didn't think she could

17

have lived through a week of not knowing if she was going to lose one of her breasts. But, at least her mother was married. Her husband wouldn't stop loving her. But if she were Laura's age, no boy would be interested in a girl with only one breast.

"Well," Laura said, "it's all over, thank goodness! Now you can forget about it—right?"

"I guess so. At least for six months. That's when I'm supposed to go back for another examination."

Charlie came into the room. "Are you okay, Mom?"

"Yes, I'm fine. Come sit down with us."

"You can sit here." Laura got up from the chair. "I have to get started on my homework." She leaned over the bed and kissed her mother on the cheek.

I love you, Mom, she wanted to say. But with Charlie there, the words wouldn't come out.

Her room was a mess. Clothes all over the floor, her bed unmade, her desk cluttered with books and papers. Every day she promised herself she would clean it up, and every day there never seemed to be enough time. Where she got her sloppy habits from, she didn't know, because her mother and father never left their things all over the place the way she did.

Well, she'd start on her French first, and maybe do a little cleaning up before she began her social studies paper.

Although she knew most of the French words that she had to translate into English, she couldn't put them together to make much sense. Thoughts of her mother kept intruding. Well, she didn't have to worry about her now. Her mother was okay. It was just a horrible scare.

*   *   *

18

The two pages were translated. It had taken longer than it usually did, but it was finished, and now, from across the hall, she could hear Charlie playing his guitar. Actually, it had been her guitar, but when she stopped playing about two years ago, he started using it, and now he played really well. Not as well as he played the piano, but he was much better than she had ever been. She got up and went to his door, where his newest funny sign was posted: STAMP OUT POVERTY. RAISE MY ALLOWANCE.

"Who dares disturb a soon-to-be genius at work?" Charlie called when she knocked.

"The genius's sister," Laura called back.

"Come in," he answered. As usual, his room was neat. There was nothing cluttering his floor or his desk. He was sitting on the edge of his bed, his guitar was on his knee, and an open music notebook was lying next to him.

He stopped playing. "What's up?"

"Nothing. I'm just taking a break. What're you playing?"

"I'm trying to figure out the harmony to a Beatles song."

"Which one?"

"'Yesterday.' It's got great chords, but they're not the ones they teach you in my harmony class, so it's kind of tricky. Listen."

Laura sat on the bed and leaned against the wall. Charlie's head was bent over the strings, his straight brown hair over his forehead, his glasses low on his nose. His voice had deepened. No more awkward cracks when he sang.

When the song was over, Charlie put down his guitar.

"That was nice," she said. "You're getting better and better."

"Thank you, thank you. You, too, can help support the Charlie Foundation of Music. Donations are gladly accepted."

19

"Sorry, no can do. I need a raise in my allowance, too." Then she said, "This thing with Mom was pretty scary, wasn't it? Did she tell you all the stuff the doctor said?"

"No. She didn't say much—except that she was glad it was over. Why? What'd she say to you?"

"She told me a little more. I guess you'd call it woman talk." She was pleased that her mother had told her more than she had told Charlie.

"In that case, I'm glad she saved that part for you," Charlie said. "My young mind might have been traumatized forever."

"Somehow I doubt that," Laura said.

"It would've been awful if something had really been wrong," Charlie said.

"I know. But everything's fine now."

"Except for our allowances," Charlie added.

They smiled at each other. "Right," Laura said.

chapter four

The next morning, riding her bike to school, Laura sang to herself as streaks of morning sunlight shone through the trees and flickered in her eyes. She rode down Ridge-view, hoping that Paul would be walking Folly. But the street was empty. Later she looked for him in the halls between her classes and at lunch in the cafeteria, but he was nowhere to be found.

For the next two weeks she rode to and from school on many different routes, always on the lookout for a golden retriever. But each day, as the leaves began to turn and the weather grew cooler, she came home disappointed.

Then one Friday afternoon in the second week of October, when the trees were bright with yellow and orange leaves, Laura saw someone walking a dog on the block ahead of her. Shifting speeds twice, she caught up with them.

"We meet again," Paul's mother said to her.

Folly sniffed Laura and wagged his long tail.

"Hi, Folly," Laura said, and leaned over to pet him. "I think you like me."

"I thinks he does, too. And you know—you've just given me an idea. But let me introduce myself. My name is Miriam Rosen."

"I'm Laura Gould," she said, and got off her bike.

"Well, Laura, I was about to put an ad in the newspaper for someone to walk Folly on Monday, Wednesday, and Friday afternoons, and since you like him so much, I was just thinking maybe you'd be interested. I'd pay thirty dollars a week. What do you think?"

Laura hesitated.

"Of course, you might not have time. Are you into all kinds of afterschool activities?"

"No, not really. I'm in the chorus, but that's on Tuesdays. Mostly I'm busy with homework. But I think I could do it. What about your son, though?"

"Paul? You mean, why can't he do it?" And then, while Folly lay down on the ground between the two of them, Mrs. Rosen explained.

She was a social worker at Harmony House, a school for severely handicapped children, and she had persuaded Paul to volunteer there three afternoons a week. "He's really good with kids," she said. "So, if you'd like the job, it's yours. What do you say?"

"Okay. I'd love to do it. When do you want me to start?"

"Could you come over on Sunday and I'll give you a key?"

"Sure," Laura said, "but maybe you'd—well—maybe you'd like a reference, or something, to be sure I'm trustworthy."

"That's nice of you to offer, but I can tell you're an honest person. I can see it in your eyes. You have lovely eyes."

Laura blushed.

"I love blue eyes. I always wanted a daughter with blue eyes and blond hair."

"Is Paul your only child?"

"Yes, he is. But even if we had a daughter, there's not much chance she'd look like you. Isidor, my husband, and I both have brown eyes and dark hair. That is, we used to. Isidor doesn't have much hair at all anymore, and these days the hairdresser keeps my hair dark."

"About Paul—" Laura began.

"Oh—you'll meet him on Sunday. Is eleven okay?"

"Eleven? Sure."

"Good." Mrs. Rosen held out her hand.

Laura shook her hand and just as she decided she'd say that she'd already met Paul, Folly and Mrs. Rosen started down the street.

Laura stopped in the doorway of the living room where Charlie and her mother were playing duets on the piano. If they stopped for a minute, she'd tell her mother about her new dog-walking job.

"Can we go a little slower?" her mother was saying to Charlie. "I know it's supposed to be allegro, but I can't play this part much faster than largo."

"Well, you'd better start practicing," Charlie said.

"I know. It's disgusting. You're so much better than I am."

"Mom—" Laura said.

Her mother turned her head toward Laura for a moment. "Hi," she said, and then looked back at the music on the piano.

"Never mind," Laura said. Partway up the stairs she saw a pile of library books on one of the steps. The title of the book on the top was *Everything You Need to Know About Breast Cancer.*

Her mother was still reading about that horrible stuff! But it was over. These books were pointless.

As she continued up the stairs, she heard Charlie and her mother laughing together.

chapter five

At breakfast Sunday morning, Laura told her parents about her dog-walking job.

"That sounds like a good thing to do," her mother said. "With the weather so nice, you'll have a chance to be outside instead of starting in on your homework right after school."

"What kind of dog is it?" her father asked.

"A golden retriever," Laura said. "He's a lovely dog."

"Aha," her father said. "Sounds like a case of puppy love to me."

Laura and her mother laughed.

"That's a good one, Dad," Laura said. "But I'd better get going. I'm supposed to be there at eleven."

Pants and shirts and sweaters were all over her floor and Laura still couldn't decide what to wear. Her favorite jeans—faded and patched—looked too sloppy. Her new ones looked—well—too new.

She pulled on a pair of last year's khaki pants. They still fit and they looked good, but the sweaters she had worn with them were a little stained and old looking. Then she remembered that Charlie had just gotten a new green shirt that would look perfect with her pants. Maybe he'd lend it to her.

The latest sign on Charlie's door was a hotel doorknob sign that her father had brought home a few weeks ago: MAID, PLEASE MAKE UP THIS ROOM.

"Come in," Charlie called when she knocked. He was sitting at his desk, his math book open in front of him. Music composition sheets were scattered all over the floor.

"Cleaning your room?" Laura asked with a laugh.

"Not a chance." Charlie motioned toward the music sheets. "I was trying to get a few notes down on the new jazz piece I'm working on, but I had to quit for homework. Do you think Mozart's dad made him do math before composing?"

"Of course," Laura said, and smiled. "But listen, I want to ask a favor."

"A favor? Like, will I let you help me with my algebra homework?"

"Right. How'd you guess?"

"I'm smart. Remember? Almost as smart as you."

It was a game they played. Charlie liked to say that she was smarter, and she would say she was only older. Laura knew they were both smart, but she got better grades than Charlie did. Grades weren't as important to him.

"Oh no. You're smarter than me," she said. "That's why you'll know what a good deal I'm going to offer you."

"Uh-oh. If you want money, forget it. I'm broke."

"It's not money. It's your shirt. The new green one. Can I borrow it? Say yes, and I'll help you do two algebra problems tonight."

"Why do you want my shirt? Where are you going?"

"Never mind. Is it a deal?"

"Only if you tell me where you're going."

"All right. I'm going to visit the family with the dog I'll be walking."

"I thought you met them."

"Some of them. But now I'm going to get to know the dog better."

"Oh, I see. You want to impress the dog with my shirt." He smiled at her. "Right?"

"Right," she said, smiling back.

"Okay," he said, and went to his closet. "Here." He handed it to her.

"Is it clean?" She held it up to her nose. It didn't smell too bad.

"Dogs like smelly things—didn't you know that? But if you want a really clean shirt—my red shirt is right out of the dryer—untouched by my fragrant bod."

"Thanks, but I like this color better." She turned to the door.

"Hey, Laura," he called after her. "I just remembered. Dogs are color blind."

"They are?" She turned back to him. "See, you *are* smarter than me. But I'll still take the shirt."

Laura wheeled her bike up the brick path to the small one-story Mediterranean-style house. Would Paul be the one to open the door? What would he say? What would she say?

A man opened the door. He was short and almost bald and wore rimless glasses. He looked too old to be Paul's father and certainly a lot older than Paul's mother.

From behind him in the house, she could hear orchestral music that sounded familiar.

"Good morning," the man said. "I think it's still morning. You must be Laura. I'm Isidor Rosen. Come in."

She followed him into the living room. It was old-fashioned-looking, with a faded Oriental rug, a large black piano, and walls lined with books. But there were books and magazines scattered all over the room. A room very different from her living room at home, where her mother kept everything in its place.

Loud music was coming from a stereo in the far end of the room. A tall stand with a large open score of music stood nearby. Mrs. Rosen sat on a couch with part of the Sunday *New York Times* on her lap. The rest of the newspaper was spread out on a square coffee table and on a big armchair next to the couch.

"Hello, Laura." Mrs. Rosen got up and cleared the papers off the chair. "Come sit down. Izz, please turn the music down."

"All right." He lowered the volume on the stereo. "But if I'm not prepared for my Carnegie Hall concert next week, you'll have to answer to Beethoven."

Beethoven. Now Laura remembered what it was. Her mother played his music often on their stereo.

"Is that the *Eroica*?" she asked timidly.

"Ah, this girl not only loves dogs," he said, "she knows music." He strode over to the music stand and came back to Laura with the score. "Can you read a music score?"

"I don't know. I can read music. I play the flute and the guitar a little—or I used to."

"Never mind 'used to.' You play the flute—my favorite instrument next to the violin, the piano, the cello, and a Mozartian soprano." He peered at her through his glasses. "And you're pretty, too."

Laura felt her face get red.

"Isidor, please! Leave the poor girl alone. You'll scare her away. And sit down before you have another heart attack. Then I'll have to get another husband, and a dog walker, too."

"Oh, all right," he said, and sat down on the couch next to Mrs. Rosen. "But I'm not finished with this girl. I've got to find out why she stopped playing the flute, and how we can get her to start again."

"Don't mind him, Laura," Mrs. Rosen said. "He's really harmless. He just gets carried away when he listens to music and thinks he's Leonard Bernstein."

"Oh, don't I wish it—Lenny—with all that hair. But I'm afraid I look more like Casals."

"Well, I'm glad you're neither of them—since they're not around anymore."

Laura was about to ask if Paul's father was a conductor when she heard the front door open and Folly came bounding into the room. He lunged at Laura, putting his big front paws in her lap.

"Hello, Folly." Laura stroked his head while his long blond tail wagged furiously back and forth. "Do you remember me?" She looked into his big dark eyes, and then she looked up and saw Paul standing in the doorway, staring at her.

"Folly, get down!" Mrs. Rosen commanded. "Paul," she continued, "this is Laura Gould."

"I know," Paul said, smiling at her now. "We've met."

"You've met?" his father asked. "You've known this lovely young woman and haven't told us one word about her?"

"Isidor, will you please shut up!" Mrs. Rosen said. She turned to Paul. "How do you know Laura?"

"Oh, it's a long, boring story," Laura said quickly. "Or rather a short, boring story." She stood up, suddenly wanting to go home. "I'm afraid I have to go now. Do you still want me to start tomorrow, Mrs. Rosen?"

"Yes. Tomorrow. And please call me Miriam."

"You can call me Isidor, which, in case you are dying to know, means gift of Isis. And of course you know who Isis was. She was the Egyptian goddess of the moon. How a Jewish baby boy gets to be called Isidor is hard to figure out. By the way—are you Jewish?"

"Dad!" Paul said.

"That's all right," Laura said. "I don't mind. Anyway, the answer is yes, I'm Jewish."

"Good," Isidor said. "I knew a girl who likes dogs, plays the flute, and knows her Beethoven has to be—"

"Isidor!" Miriam said. "Please! You're such a chauvinist!" She turned to Laura. "Here, I almost forgot. Take the key."

"Thanks." Laura put the key in her jacket pocket.

Paul followed her into the hallway and opened the front door for her. "I guess my father was putting on one of his performances for you," he said softly.

"You mean his conducting?" Laura asked.

"No. The other stuff. The 'lovely young girl' bit."

"Oh, that. Yeah, a little."

"Well, he's not really like that."

"What do you mean?"

"I mean—he's not really—well, always joking and

pretending to flirt. He's really different." Suddenly looking sad, he said, "He's really a great guy. But my mother and I are worried about him. He had a heart attack about six months ago."

"Oh, I'm sorry. Was it a bad one?"

"Yeah. Pretty bad. That's why we moved to the suburbs. We used to live in a great brownstone in the city, but it was a three-story walk-up and a long subway ride to his store. He's a pharmacist—and a friend offered him a partnership in a drugstore in Yonkers. So we bought this house that's all on one floor. It's much easier for him here."

"I hope he'll be okay now," Laura said. "I like him. I like your mother, too."

"Listen, you told me you like my father, and you like my mother, but you didn't tell me if you like Folly." Paul had a teasing look as he smiled at her.

"Oh, I *love* Folly." She laughed. "Well, I'll see you," she said, and went out the door.

chapter six

At school on Monday, Laura kept slipping her hand into the back pocket of her jeans to be sure the key to Paul's house was still there. Each time she touched it, she added another small part to the story she was imagining.

She would find Paul in the kitchen, waiting for her with Folly. He'd smile shyly and she'd say, "What are you doing here? Aren't you supposed to be at Harmony House?"

"I know," he'd say, "but I switched with a friend."

"How come?" she'd say.

"Oh, I just thought maybe I ought to be here—your first day on the job—you know. I thought I'd show you some of Folly's favorite trees and bushes."

And then they'd take Folly out together. They'd walk slowly down the street, maybe over to her block. She'd show him where she lived.

Of course when she got to Paul's house, only Folly was there to greet her. He barked at the sound of her key in the lock and leaped up at her when she opened the kitchen door. His tail loudly thumped the floor as he tried to lick her face.

"Hey, Folly, old fella," she said, pushing him away. "Calm down and be a good boy."

His leash was on the table. Next to it was a note. She thought it might be for her, but it said:

Paul—I'll be a little late. Don't forget to call Dr. Berman. And please try to get Dad to take a nap before dinner, but don't tell him I said you should.

Laura attached Folly's leash to his collar and opened the kitchen door. Folly lunged outside, pulling her after him.

That night Laura's mother suggested that the two of them go out for dinner. Charlie was having dinner at a friend's, and her father was working late. Laura was surprised. They'd never done this before—just the two of them—and on a school night.

"And you can pick," her mother said. "Chinese, French, Italian. I'm game for anything. Even Indian."

"Gee, I don't know," Laura said. "What would you like?"

"Someplace different. Someplace we wouldn't go to with Dad and Charlie."

"That means a place with seafood."

"Hey, how about that Japanese place in Hartsdale?"

"Okay," Laura said.

When they were in the restaurant with its modern black-and-white decor, Laura ordered shrimp tempura and a Coke. Her mother ordered sushi and a bottle of Japanese beer.

"Want to try some of mine?" her mother asked when their food arrived. Laura reached over and took a portion of the raw fish and rice.

Eating it with the sharp-tasting ginger and mustard, the fish didn't seem to have much flavor of its own.

"What do you think?" her mother asked.

"It's okay. Want to try my shrimp?"

"Thanks," her mother said. "Hey, wouldn't it be nice to go to a different restaurant every night? I think I'll suggest it to Dad."

"And then he'll ask what you've been drinking." Laura giggled. "You're really feeling good, aren't you, Mom?"

"Yes, I am. I'm feeling lucky. The good news from the doctor was like a reprieve. At first I just felt this huge relief after all that worrying, but now—I don't know—I just feel terrific. Maybe you have to go through something like this to know what I'm talking about."

Laura nodded.

"The worst part, of course, was being afraid I had cancer—and the awful things that could mean. If the news was bad, I was wondering how we would all deal with it."

"I know, Mom. But Charlie and I aren't little kids anymore. If you were sick for a while, we'd manage. We'd even take care of you. I'll bet you can't imagine that happening, can you?"

"Please—let's not even think about that," her mother said, and laughed. "Now I want to hear about you. Tell me about your dog-walking job."

"Well, I just started it. But he's a beautiful dog. His name is Folly."

"Folly?"

"Yes. There's a story that goes with the name that Mrs. Rosen told me. I mean Miriam. She told me to call her that.

And Mr. Rosen—he told me to call him Isidor. He's a real character. He loves music and he loves to tell jokes and—"

"And I guess you like them. That's nice." Her mother's voice was suddenly tight and flat. "Do they have any children?"

"Yes, they have a son, Paul. He does volunteer work at Harmony House three afternoons a week. That's when they need me to walk the dog."

"Well, they're lucky to have found someone responsible like you." She put her hand over Laura's. "But I'm the really lucky one—having you for a daughter. My poor mother never had a chance to see *her* daughter growing up."

"How much do you remember about your mother?" Laura asked.

"Not much, really. I was only five when she died. Everyone said I looked like her. We were both blond—like you."

Laura looked at her mother's hair. Now it was almost a faded brown, with streaks of gray here and there.

"Your mother was so young when she died," Laura said.

"Only thirty. Really only a little bit younger than I am now. I know what it's like to not have a mother. That's why I was so terrified for you and Charlie when I thought I might have cancer."

"Dad hasn't talked much about all of this," Laura said. "If you hadn't told us about it that night at dinner, we would never have known."

"I know," her mother said. "He doesn't like to talk about painful things."

"Does it bother you that he talks so little?"

"Sometimes. I think he's really a shy person. Even though I wish Dad would talk more, there's a lot of love he shows without words."

Laura nodded.

"Hey, enough serious talk. We're here to celebrate." She picked up her beer glass and raised it. "To happy, healthy days for all of us."

The next afternoon when Laura was at her desk doing homework, her mother came into her room with a sheet of paper in her hand.

"I hope Dad doesn't mind my showing you this—but after what we talked about last night, I thought this might help you to understand him a little better."

Laura took the paper from her mother. "I didn't know Dad wrote poetry."

Laura read:

FILLING CORNERS, FILLING MOMENTS.

He silent, she unable to bear silence;
She talks, he cannot bear talk.

She silent, unable to bear silence
He talking, unable to bear talking.

He talks to please her;
She is silent to please him.

She fills the moments with music;
He, loving her, loves music.

She fills all corners, all moments;
He empties all moments, all corners.

She gathers, he deletes;
She turns out, he turns in.

She smiles, he smiles;
Love lingers in the corners.
Love lingers in the moments.

"That's really nice," Laura said. "I can see why he gave it to you. Has he written other poems?"

"Yes. He writes whenever he has some free time."

Laura read the poem one more time. "Why doesn't he show me his writing, too?"

"Because he doesn't think it's very good," her mother said. "But maybe he'll show you if you ask."

"It'd be nicer if I didn't have to," Laura said.

"I know."

On Wednesday, there was another note from Miriam on the Rosens' kitchen table:

Laura—Could you come on Thursday—tomorrow—instead of Friday?

There was a pencil next to the note.

Laura had made plans to go shopping with Rachel on Thursday, but she thought she could persuade Rachel to change it to Friday. She wrote: "Yes. Fine."

After finishing her walk with Folly, she was surprised to see both her parents' cars in the driveway. Her father was home early.

Charlie was sitting at the kitchen table, eating a dish of chocolate pudding.

"How come Dad's home?" Laura asked.

"He went to the doctor with Mom." Charlie looked pale and scared. "She has to go to the hospital."

"What are you talking about? What's wrong?"

"The doctor said she has to have a piece of the lump taken out to be sure it's okay."

Laura stared at him. "Where is Mom?" she asked, suddenly shivering.

"Upstairs. She's taking a nap. Dad's in the den."

Her father was at his desk with one of his law journals open in front of him.

"What's going on, Dad? I thought everything was okay with Mommy." As she heard her words, she realized she hadn't called her mother Mommy for years.

"Well, it probably is. But Mom read this book and decided to see another doctor—to be absolutely sure. He said to be really safe, she should have a biopsy."

Biopsy. She knew that word. It was a word that you used with people who might have cancer. "When is she going to do it?"

"Monday—at Mount Sinai in New York. I'm going with her."

"How long will she be there?"

"Just that day. It's an outpatient procedure."

"And when will you know if—well, if it's okay?"

"We'll get the pathologist's first report the same day. And then a few days later, we'll get a more definite report."

"Oh, Daddy—" She wanted to hear him say, "It's going to be all right." But he looked away and turned a pen around and around between his fingers.

"That first doctor is a really big wheel," her father said. "He's head of the department. I'm sure he knew what he was talking about. She'll be okay."

On Thursday, when Laura opened the Rosens' kitchen door, Folly was not there to greet her.

"Folly!" she called, her voice echoing in the empty house. "Folly!" She heard faint sounds from the other end of the house. She walked slowly past the living room and down a long hall. The first two doors were closed, but the one door beyond them was open, and there was Folly stretched out on the floor next to an unmade bed. He looked up at her with sleepy eyes and slowly got up, stretching his long, golden body and giving a big, toothy yawn.

"Well, there you are, old lazybones."

Folly ambled over to her, then he lay down again at her feet, his tail softly thumping on the carpet.

It was obviously Paul's room. There were posters on the wall and a stereo on top of a bookcase filled with books and tapes and CDs.

In front of the window was his desk, cluttered like hers with schoolbooks and a big loose-leaf notebook. Laura went over to it and opened the notebook.

He was taking pretty much the same courses she was. She was just about to close the notebook when she saw two words in blue ink: *Dear Laura.*

That was all.

She stared at the page until she heard a car driving by outside. Quickly, she closed the notebook and turned back to Folly.

"Okay, Folly, let's go," she said.

They started on the same route she had taken the two

previous days. Folly had taken the lead before, stopping when he wanted to, but mostly pulling her ahead. Now she found herself tugging at his leash, urging him to move faster. For a long time he sniffed a telephone pole that must have been the favorite of countless dogs. Two words kept racing through her head: *Dear Laura.*

Miriam's car was in the driveway when Laura returned with Folly. She found Miriam and Paul sitting at the kitchen table. Miriam was having a cup of tea. Paul had a can of Coke.

Dear Laura. Dear Laura.

"I didn't realize it was so late," she said. "You know, Folly was a real slowpoke today."

"I told you, Mom," Paul said. "He's really getting worse."

"All right. I believe you," Miriam said. "Anyway, we'll see what Dr. Berman says tomorrow."

"What's wrong with Folly?" Laura asked.

"Paul, you explain," Miriam said, getting up. "I'm bushed. I'm going to lie down for a while before I start dinner." She took her cup and saucer with her and left the kitchen.

"You want something to drink?" Paul asked Laura. He opened the refrigerator.

"Sure." She sat down at the table. "But tell me about Folly."

Paul handed her a can of soda and then sat down opposite her. "Well, Dr. Berman isn't sure what's wrong with him, but he isn't eating like he used to. Some days he seems to be okay—like his old self, but some days—like today—he drags around like he's dying. So we're taking him back to the vet tomorrow and he's going to do some tests over the weekend."

He leaned down to stroke Folly who was lying peacefully at his feet. "You'd better be all right, you dumb dog."

"He will be," Laura said.

Sunday night Laura stood by the window in her darkened bedroom. At dinner Charlie had said something about it being a clear night for stars, and now she was looking at a sky filled with tiny crystal lights while she wrote a letter in her head.

Dear Paul. Are you finishing your letter to me?

There was a knock and her door opened.

"Hi," her mother said. "Why are your lights out?"

"Charlie was right," Laura said. "Look at the stars. Come see. There must be billions—no—trillions of them."

Her mother stood next to her and suddenly they saw a shooting star speeding downward. Then, just as it disappeared, a second star streaked after it.

"Wow! Two shooting stars," her mother said. "That means we get two wishes. One for each of us." She put her arm around Laura's shoulder. "What do you wish?"

Laura was thinking about Paul.

"Well, there's no secret to what I'm wishing now," her mother said.

How could she be thinking about Paul when her mother needed her wish? "I wish the same thing, Mom."

"Thank you, sweetie. I know you do." She turned away from the window. "I want to talk to you about tomorrow. Okay?"

"Sure," Laura said, and switched on her desk light.

"I should be home in the late afternoon, but I think I'll be kind of knocked out. I think Dad's going to be pretty wiped out, too. So if you could keep an eye on Charlie and just take charge of things . . ."

"Of course I will. Do you want me to cook something? I can't cook like you, but—"

"You don't need to cook anything. Dad's going to order in—Chinese or pizza—when we get home. Or maybe something fancier, if the pathologist's report is good and we have something to celebrate."

"Oh, Mom, I sure hope we will."

"Me, too, sweetie. But even if the report is bad, I still have some choices. I can probably have a lumpectomy instead of mastectomy. They just take out the lump. If it's cancer—and it hasn't spread to your nodes—then they usually give your breast radiation treatment, but they don't remove it."

Breast—remove. Laura didn't want to hear those words. "A lumpectomy sounds good, Mom. Would you do that?"

"I don't know. But I'd certainly consider it—if I have to. A lot of women have them. Right now I just need to get through the next few days." She put her hand on Laura's shoulder. "I can't believe this is happening to me."

"Me, neither." Her mother's eyes filled with tears. Laura put her arms around her and held her close, feeling the soft fullness of her mother's breasts against her own. Her throat felt tight and she swallowed hard, but no tears would come.

"It's going to be all right, Mom," she said softly. "I'm sure it is."

chapter seven

Monday afternoon Laura rode her bike toward the Rosens' house. Her legs were pushing the pedals. Her eyes saw that some of the trees were already bare, and some had leaves that had turned to orange and red. But she couldn't feel a thing.

Words like *mastectomy* and *lumpectomy* swirled around in her mind, like words from a foreign language. They had nothing to do with her. All she wanted was to take Folly for a very short walk and then go home. She wanted to be there before her mother came home from the hospital.

Her father was in the kitchen talking to Charlie when she got home.

"Dad!" Laura said, dumping her backpack on the table. "I didn't think you'd be here so soon. Where's Mom?"

"She's upstairs, resting," her father said.

"How is she?"

"She's okay."

"She is? Really? That's great."

"No—I mean—she's all right. But—"

"But what?"

"But that first doctor was a jerk," Charlie said. "She's got cancer."

"Oh no," Laura said. "Is that true, Dad?"

"That's what the pathologist's report said."

"But what about the other report—the one you get a few days later?"

"That one is usually the same if the first one says the lump is malignant."

"But what about what that other doctor said?"

"Sometimes doctors make mistakes. It's a good thing she saw someone else, or she'd really be in trouble."

"You should sue that first guy," Charlie said.

"I can't think about that now," her father said. "Listen—what do you kids want for supper? Pizza or Chinese?"

"Pizza," Charlie said.

"Pizza okay with you, Laura?" her father asked.

"Sure. Whatever."

In the hour before dinner, Laura sat at her desk, trying to do her homework. But soon she pushed aside her math book and opened her dictionary.

> **cancer:** n. **1.a.** A malignant tumor that tends to invade healthy tissue and spread to new sites. **b.** The pathological condition characterized by such growths. **2.** A pernicious, spreading evil.

She looked up another word.

malignant. adj. **1.** Showing great malevolence. **2.** Highly injurious. **3.** Designating a pathological growth that tends to spread.

She already knew the meaning of all those words. She should be studying for her math test.

Tends to spread...A pernicious, spreading evil... Her mother's cancer could spread—even when the tumor was removed. There was a girl in her homeroom, Leslie Miller, someone she knew only slightly, whose mother had died of cancer last year. Maybe it had started in her breast. She'd ask someone at school who knew Leslie. No. She wouldn't do that.

She wouldn't tell anyone, except Rachel.

Maybe Rachel would know about some of the newest treatments for breast cancer from her parents' medical journals. Both of her parents were doctors. Maybe there was some new cure that her own mother hadn't heard about yet.

She opened her math book again and tried to concentrate. Soon she heard Charlie playing the piano.

The music drifting up to her was beautiful. Listening to the slow, sad melody, she envied Charlie. She pictured him sitting at the piano, his long fingers moving across the keys, the music flowing softly, softly—almost like the tears that she wished she could shed.

The doorbell rang and the music stopped.

"Laura," her father called. "The pizza's here."

"I'll be right down," Laura said. "Is Mom going to eat with us?"

"No, she says she's not hungry."

"Can I go in and see her now?"

"Sure, but come down a minute first. You can bring her the cup of tea I made her."

Her mother was sitting up on her bed, a blue afghan spread across her legs.

"Oh, Laura—thanks, sweetheart. I'm so glad to see you."

"I'm glad to see you, too." Laura set the cup of tea down on the night table. She leaned over to give her a hug.

Her mother put her arms around Laura and held her close. "Can you sit down for a while?"

"Sure." Laura sat in the big chair next to the bed while her mother sipped her tea. "Mom, I'm so sorry."

"I know, sweetie. It's awful."

"It sure is."

"How are you feeling? Does it hurt where they did the biopsy?"

"No, that feels okay. It's just a little tender. It's what happens next that has me—" She stopped, and tears rolled down her cheeks. "Life sure is unpredictable, isn't it."

Laura's throat swelled up. All she could do was nod in agreement. She reached for her mother's hand, and then, at last, her own tears came. Not the hot outpouring that she longed for, but at least something was finally coming through.

She knelt down at the side of the bed and put her head in her mother's lap. Her mother softly stroked her hair.

chapter eight

"That was an impossible test," Laura said as she finished the last of her tuna fish sandwich.

"Yeah, it was pretty hard," Rachel said. She was eating a salad of bean sprouts, carrots, and tofu.

"*Pretty* hard?" Laura said. "I'm sure I messed it up. I couldn't remember half the stuff—and I really studied for it. I was up past midnight."

"Listen, you had a few other things on your mind last night. Why don't you tell Mrs. Richards about your mother? She'd understand. Maybe she'll let you take the test over."

"No," Laura said quickly. "I don't want to do that. I'm not telling anyone besides you. Remember that. Don't tell Nancy or Amy. No one."

"Okay," Rachel said. "I guess I should have asked you first, but after you called last night I told my mother."

"That's okay. I meant people at school. What did she say?"

"Well, of course she was really sorry. She told me to tell you that. But she also said that lumpectomies are just as safe for most women now. Mastectomies are hardly performed at all anymore."

"Really?" Laura said. She took a deep breath and felt something inside her loosen.

When she came to take Folly out, she found him sleeping in a patch of sunlight on the kitchen floor.

Before she got Folly's leash, she went into Paul's room quickly and looked at his desk. No notebook. Just a bunch of schoolbooks. On his dresser was an open blue cookie can half filled with pennies. Next to it were some folded shirts.

And then she saw his notebook on his bed, almost in front of her nose. This time, there was a half page of writing.

Dear Laura,

I'll bet you're surprised to be getting a letter from me— especially since I could call you. Well, I thought I'd keep this boring French class from being a total loss by writing this lettre à toi. (Tu? Vous? Je ne sais pas.) If only I had learned a little more French this year, I'd write it all en français, and then you'd realize how brilliant and fantastic I am. Mais, il est impossible.

What a lot of boring boloney you're going to think this is if I'm ever stupid enough to send it to you. But since I know you're not really interested in hearing from me, I'm not. (Mailing it, that is. Stupid, I am.)

He likes me! He likes me! She wanted to sing it out loud as she went back to the kitchen.

"Come on, old boy." She put on Folly's leash and he slowly got to his feet.

As they walked their familiar route she let him stop wherever he wanted.

"Hey, Folly, did you know that Paul likes me?" she said when he sat down at the edge of the road. "Isn't that great?"

He sniffed a pile of leaves.

Well, Folly wasn't impressed. But then again, he was just a dumb dog. And Paul was pretty dumb, too, if he really thought that she didn't like him. She'd have to find a way to let him know. Maybe she'd call him. Yes, she'd think of some reason that she needed to call him—tonight.

Paul was sitting at the table drinking a glass of orange juice when Laura pulled Folly into the kitchen. "What are you doing here?" she said.

"I have a horrible sore throat, so they told me to go home. I called Mom and she said I should drink this." He lifted his glass. "It's full of Vitamin C and it's supposed to make me feel better, but it doesn't."

"That's too bad," she said. She bent down to take off Folly's leash, and when she straightened up, Paul was staring at her. She blushed and he looked away.

"I've been meaning to ask you," Laura said, sitting down on the chair next to him. "What did the vet say about Folly? Did they find out what's wrong with him?"

"He has a tumor in his stomach. The vet said it's probably malignant."

"Your dog has cancer?" First her mother—and now Folly.

"That's what malignant means."

"I know what malignant means. I was just surprised, that's all. What are you going to do?"

"Well, Dr. Berman said he could be operated on, but the chances of his surviving the operation aren't so great, so for now we're going to wait and see how he does."

"That's really too bad. How old is Folly?"

"Seven. That's like forty-nine for a person."

Suddenly Laura thought about her mother at home, feeling scared and sad.

"Listen, I've got to go." She stood up. "I'll see you."

Her mother was reading in her bedroom.

"Hi, sweetheart. How's the dog walking going?"

"Fine," Laura said. She wouldn't tell her that Folly had cancer, too. "What're you reading?"

"It's another book on breast cancer. I have to decide what to do, because apparently lumpectomies aren't safe with certain kinds of tumors."

"What does your doctor say you should do?"

"He says that with the type of tumor I have, it would be safer for me to have a mastectomy."

"Oh, Mom, how are you going to decide?"

"Well, one thing I've learned from this gruesome experience is that you should always get a second opinion. I may even get a third."

"What does Dad think you should do?"

"He says it's up to me, but I know he wants me to have a mastectomy." She stopped for a moment. "I know he wants the best for me, but I don't think a man can really know how I'm feeling. The thought of losing my breast if it's not necessary . . ."

"That would be terrible," Laura said.

"I know. But if it would mean I'd be safer—I was looking forward to being a grandmother one day." She looked at Laura with a sad smile. "I know you're going to have lovely children."

Laura opened her French book and stared blankly at the pages. She couldn't stop thinking about her mother's choices. If she were in her mother's place, she knew she'd take a chance and have the lumpectomy. She'd never want to say to a boy who was about to put his hand under her sweater, "Wait a minute—there's something I need to tell you. . . ."

But she knew it didn't happen to young girls. Still, it *could* happen to her someday. She had read in a magazine that daughters of women who have had breast cancer are more likely to have it than other women.

She looked down at the page in her French book. The words were a jumble.

And then she remembered her plan to call Paul. Yes, she'd call to see how he was feeling. It must have seemed weird, running off like she did. Certainly unfriendly. That might have convinced him that she *didn't* like him.

It was only nine o'clock when she went downstairs to use the kitchen phone. The house seemed unusually quiet. Dinner had been quiet, too. What little conversation there was had been about the Chinese food her father had brought home, that is until her mother read her fortune cookie.

"'Be of good cheer,'" she had read aloud. "'You are a winner.'" She took the narrow strip of paper and started tearing it into little pieces. "What jerk writes these stupid things?"

"Listen, sweetheart," her father said, and put his hand on her mother's. "You'll be a winner. I know you will."

Her mother shrugged and was silent.

Looking at the kitchen phone now, Laura realized she didn't know Paul's number. It wasn't in the local phone book, probably because they had moved too recently. She called information and then stared at the number she'd written down. Finally, taking a deep breath, she dialed.

Paul picked up on the first ring.

"Hello."

"Hi. It's me. Laura."

"Oh. Hi."

"How's your throat?" she asked. "Is it still sore?"

"Yeah, it's awful. It kills me just to swallow."

"Really? What did you do about dinner?"

"My mother made me some chicken soup."

"Of course. That's what every good mother gives her sick kid."

"So—" he said, and then laughed.

"So—" she said, and laughed, too. "I suppose you're wondering why I called."

"Sort of—although I'm not fussy. There doesn't have to be a reason."

"Well—actually—I called to apologize for leaving so suddenly when you were telling me about Folly. I'm really sorry about him having—having that tumor."

"Yeah. It is kind of awful. I keep hoping the vet is wrong."

"Well, doctors do make mistakes. Big mistakes."

"I know. Anyway, something is certainly wrong with him. I just hope nothing happens before I go on my school trip. My social studies class is going to Colonial Williamsburg."

"Really? How long will you be gone?"

"About a week. I'll be back next Sunday afternoon."

A week? She didn't say anything for a moment, afraid that her voice would betray her disappointment.

"Well, send me a postcard, okay?" she said at last.

"Sure. And, Laura—"

What, what, what? "Yeah?"

"You really are psychic. You read my mind tonight. I was thinking of calling you."

"You were? I mean—uh—I know. I mean—oh, I don't know what I mean."

"Never mind. Listen—I'll see you when I get back. I'll call you. Okay?"

"Okay. I mean—great!"

Finally, somehow, the conversation came to an end, and then Laura was back in her room. She took her pillow in her arms and danced around and around to the music on her stereo.

chapter nine

Paul had been gone five days, but it had seemed like a month. Her mother's decision was still unmade. A few days ago she had gone to a doctor in New York, and today she was going to New York again to see another doctor. Her mother's friend Ruth Fisher had had a mastectomy a year ago, and now she was over at the house every day when her mother came home from teaching. The two of them spent hours talking together about her mother's choices.

Walking Folly was the only thing that took Laura's mind off her mother's cancer, especially now that she'd promised herself not to snoop in Paul's room again.

Right now Folly was pulling her toward a squirrel that was scrambling up a tree. The squirrel disappeared into the mass of yellow leaves at the top of the tree, and Folly lay down and closed his eyes.

"Come on, old dog," she said, pulling on his leash. "It's time to go back. I think you need a nap, and I need to get home." She had a biology test the next day. But Folly kept stopping. He lay down several times on each block.

As she approached the Rosens' house, she saw a car in the driveway.

Music was coming from the living room, and then Isidor appeared in the doorway, an amber-colored drink in his hand. He was wearing slippers and a gray wool cardigan.

"Well, well, well," he said. "Laura, what a nice surprise."

"Hi," Laura said. "It's my day to walk Folly."

"Oh, that's right. I forgot. It must be nice walking outside now—with the leaves so beautiful."

"Yes, it is. The colors are wonderful."

"I envy you," Isidor said. "I was never an athlete, but I did love walking. Miriam and I used to take long walks all over the city. I was hoping we'd be able to do it out here, too."

"Maybe you'll be able to again," Laura said.

"Maybe. The doctor says that if I behave myself—and I'm lucky—I might. Meanwhile, I'm allowed one drink a day— it's even supposed to be good for me. And, of course, I have my music."

"I like what you're playing. What is it?"

"It's a Mozart piano concerto. Number 23 in A major. The second movement has one of the saddest and most beautiful melodies that was ever written. And speaking of sad things, how is our poor decrepit Folly getting along?" He stroked Folly, who was lying at his feet.

"Not so good. He's really a slowpoke when I take him out."

Isidor gently swirled the liquor in his glass, then smiled at her. "Can I offer you some refreshment? A glass of something?

You're too young for the joys of Johnnie Walker, but I'm sure Paul has something suitable."

"No, thanks. I've really got to get going. I've got tons of homework."

"Ah, too bad. With Paul away, I miss the patter of big feet." He sat down at the table. "I guess I'll finish my drink and then take a little nap before the good wife returns."

"Are you feeling all right? I mean—you're not sick, are you?"

"No. But I didn't feel a hundred percent this afternoon, so my partner told me to go home. Insisted, as a matter of fact. He's a bit of a worrywart. Like Miriam. Sure you won't stay awhile?" He looked so sad and lonely.

"I wish I could," Laura said, moving toward the door. "Maybe another time."

As she rode her bike toward home, she wished she could have forgotten about her homework just this once.

A postcard from Paul was waiting for her when she reached home. On one side was a picture of the ocean and boardwalk at Asbury Park. On the other side Paul had written:

> Dear Laura,
>   Would you believe we've just passed a town called Wannamassa? All I can think of is no, I don't wannamassa.
>   How's Folly? How's Laura?
>   Love, Paul
>   (social scientist and historical researcher)

She read the postcard three times. He had written "love."

*   *   *

She was deep into her homework when her mother came into her room.

"What's the matter?" Laura asked. "You look awful."

"I've made my decision. That's what's the matter. I'm going to have the mastectomy."

Laura's stomach tightened into a cold knot, and she had to swallow hard before she could speak. "Is that what the doctor you saw today recommended?"

"Yes. He said that the tumor I have is aggressive and it might be spreading."

"To where?"

"My lymph nodes. They'll be checking them during the surgery. My other doctor recommended a mastectomy, too."

Laura took a deep breath. "When are you going to do it?" she asked finally.

"On Monday morning."

"When can I come to see you in the hospital?"

"Wednesday. I'd love to see you and Charlie then. Okay?"

"Sure."

Her mother sat down on Laura's bed. "Listen, honey, I know this whole thing is upsetting to you, but you know that this almost never happens to young women—in case you're worried about this happening to you."

"I'm not worried," Laura said, looking away.

"That's good, because by the time you get to be my age, I'm sure they'll have already found a cure for this stupid disease."

"Mom—" Laura focused on the tiny words of her textbook.

"What?"

"I've got this test tomorrow—"

"Oh, sorry. I guess I've been going on and on." She got up and went out of the room.

Laura turned back to her book with a sick feeling of shame. She had sounded so cold—even uninterested. She thought of calling her mother to come back, but she couldn't. She just couldn't bear talking about it anymore.

chapter ten

All Sunday evening Laura waited for Paul to call. He'd said he'd call her when he got back from Willliamsburg, but the phone was busy with calls from her parents' friends, everyone wishing her mother good luck with her surgery. Laura tried to work on an English essay on her computer, but her mind kept wandering back and forth between her mother and Paul. Finally, she gave up and watched an old movie on TV.

Around nine her mother came into the den and sat down on the couch next to Laura. She was in her nightgown and bathrobe.

Laura switched off the TV. "You're going to bed already?" she asked her mother.

"Yes, I've got to be up really early. I'm scheduled for seven o'clock."

"Seven?"

"I know. In the old days I hear you went in the night before—and they let you stay about a week. But not anymore."

Finally Laura said, "It just seems so awful."

"I know," her mother said, and then almost in a whisper, she said, "Laura—"

"What, Mom?"

"I love you. Very much. Remember that."

"I love you, too, Mom." And then Laura couldn't speak.

"I'll talk to you tomorrow night," her mother said, and took Laura in her arms.

That night Laura dreamed about rows of closed doors in a hospital, and she woke crying out, "Mom! Mom!" The room was dark and it was several minutes before her heart stopped racing.

Her clock read ten to three. She got out of bed and went to her parents' room.

Only her mother was in the big bed, sound asleep on her side.

She went out into the hall and looked down the stairs. A pale light came from the den. She made her way slowly through the dark house and found her father sitting on the couch in front of the TV. A black-and-white movie was on, but the sound was turned off. He looked up at her. Tears were running down his cheeks. She went over to him and sat down. He put his arm around her and they sat there together, staring at the silent screen.

Monday night, while she and Charlie were having supper, she called the hospital. Her father answered and said that everything had gone well. When her mother got on the phone, her voice was slow and slurred. It was because of the anesthesia, she explained, but she said she felt all right since they had given her some medicine for the pain. Mostly she was just sleepy.

Later, when the phone had finally stopped ringing with calls from her parents' friends, Laura dialed Paul's number.

"Hi, Mrs. Rosen—I mean Miriam. It's Laura. Laura Gould."

"Oh, hello, Laura. How are you?"

"I'm fine. But I won't be able to come over on Wednesday to walk Folly. I'm awfully sorry."

"Oh, that's all right. Wednesday. Let's see. I'll work something out. Don't worry about it. Isidor told me he saw you the other day when he came home early."

"Yes. How is he? Is he feeling better?"

"A little better. He just needs to learn to take it easy. He enjoyed seeing you. Stop by sometimes. I'd love to see you, too."

"Thanks, I'll try to do that. Uh—is Paul home? I mean, could I speak to him?"

"Sure. I'll get him."

While she waited, she tried to remember the words she had rehearsed to herself up in her room.

"I can't believe it," Paul said. "I've been trying to call you since yesterday. I even asked the operator to see if your number was out of order, but she said you were talking."

"It wasn't me, believe me. We used to have call waiting, but after a while my mother couldn't stand it, so now we don't have it. By the way, thanks for the card."

"You're welcome. So how come your phone's been so busy?

"My mother's in the hospital. She's probably coming home on Thursday, but I'm visiting her in the hospital on Wednesday. That's why I can't walk Folly then."

"Your mother's in the hospital? What's wrong?"

"She had an operation—and millions of people have been calling to see how she's doing."

61

"Oh, that explains it. Is she okay? I mean—what kind of operation did she have, or is it none of my business?"

She was prepared for that question. "It's a female kind of thing," she said, hoping he'd think her mother had had a hysterectomy. Those were the words she had heard one of her mother's friends say to Charlie about a woman who'd had her uterus removed.

"Oh, my mother had that," Paul said. "A long time ago. That's why I'm an only child."

"I didn't know that."

"There are lots of things you don't know about me, Miss Psychic. You must be losing your powers. Do you know, for example, how my class trip was?"

"No, I don't. Are you going to tell me?"

"Not on the phone. I think that requires person-to-person contact."

"Oh. Okay. What did you have in mind?"

"Oh, I don't know. I thought we'd go out together—maybe go to a movie. How does that sound to you?"

"That sounds good."

"Just good? I was hoping for fantastic."

"Oh. Well, how about terrific?"

"Almost as good. How about Saturday night?"

"Fantastic."

chapter eleven

How will she look? How will she look?

That was all Laura could think about as she walked down the hospital corridor to her mother's room. She glanced at Charlie, walking beside her. He had to be worried about that, too. He had been unusually quiet in Ruth's car on the drive into the city. Ruth had done most of the talking, telling them about how hard the whole thing was for their mother now, but that it wouldn't be long before she was back to her old self. "Look at me," she had said. "I'm doing everything I ever did."

"Laura! Charlie!" Her mother held out one arm to them. "It's so good to see you."

"Hi, Mom." Laura hugged her mother awkwardly, afraid of hurting her. Then she moved away to make room for Charlie.

Her mother's nightgown was loosely gathered on top, and with no bandages showing, you couldn't really tell that there was anything wrong, anything different.

"Where's Ruth?" her mother asked.

"She's looking for a parking space," Laura said.

"Hey, your own TV," Charlie said, "and a view of the park. This is a great room."

"I have Dad to thank for all this luxury. He insisted I have a private room."

"You look good, Mom," Laura said. "How do you feel?"

"Not too bad, considering. I get tired. I guess I'm still a little weak."

"Which side is it?" Charlie asked.

"Charlie!" Laura said sharply.

"That's okay," her mother said. "It's the right side."

"How's the food here?" Charlie asked.

"Not bad. How's the food at home?"

"Terrible," Charlie said. "I'm thinking about calling Child Protective Services before I'm poisoned." Their mother laughed.

"I made a tuna casserole last night that was pretty good," Laura said.

"If you like tuna fish," Charlie said.

"Well, you don't like anything. Anyway, it's your turn to cook tonight. What're you making?"

"Tonight Dad's taking us to Burger King. I, Chef Charlie, am cooking my masterpiece tomorrow. Chicken pot pies!"

"That's not cooking," Laura said. "That shouldn't count."

"Says who?"

"Says me. Anyone can stick a frozen dinner in the oven."

"Hey, you two," her mother said. "Cut it out."

"Sorry," Laura said.

"When are you coming home?" Charlie asked.

"Maybe tomorrow."

"Are you allowed out of bed yet?" Laura asked.

"Oh, sure. I get up to go to the bathroom and last night I took a walk down the hall with Dad. And when Ruth comes up, I'm going to ask her to wash my hair in the bathroom sink. I can't stand the way it looks when I haven't washed it for a couple of days, and I won't be allowed to take a shower for at least a week or two—when the bandages come off."

She talked about it so calmly. And she looked so normal— as though nothing terrible had happened. But something terrible *had* happened.

"Your hair looks fine to me," Charlie said.

"Thanks, but I don't think so," her mother said. "Ruth thinks I ought to start coloring it—to get it looking blond again. What do you think?"

"Go for it Mom," Charlie said.

"Do it," Laura said. "I think it's a good idea."

And then Ruth came into the room, and Laura leaned back in her chair. Now she could relax. Ruth would know all the right things to say.

That night, before going to bed, Laura took off her bra and looked at herself in the mirror over her dresser. She had nice breasts. Not too full and not too small. But if she had only one breast, she'd look lopsided and horrible. She turned away from the mirror.

Her mother came home from the hospital the next day. She spent most of the time resting in bed, coming down to eat with them the take-out meal their father picked up on his way home from work. Friends came to visit with casseroles and gifts of flowering plants and books. Ruth brought a roast chicken and everything to go with it.

On Saturday night Miriam drove Paul and Laura to the movies in Greenburgh.

"I'll sure be glad when I'm sixteen," Laura said to Paul as Miriam drove away and they stood on line to get their tickets. "Don't you hate having to be driven everywhere by your parents?"

"I don't know. It's not so bad. But my mother says she can't wait for me to get my learner's permit next week. I'll be sixteen on Friday."

"No kidding. You mean I'm going out with an older man?"

"I guess so. When's your birthday?"

"Not until February. Months away."

"Oh, you're just a child. I'd better be careful."

She smiled at him because, of course, he was joking. But now the movie was half over, and he still hadn't taken her hand or put his arm around her shoulder.

In the car, coming to the movies, he had talked almost nonstop about his class trip.

But in the darkened theater, Paul was like a different person. After they had finished sharing a container of popcorn, he had slumped down in his seat and became totally absorbed in the movie. He didn't seem to know that she was sitting next to him with her hand resting in her lap, just waiting for him to reach for it.

She turned to look at Paul now. He caught her glance and smiled at her, and a small flame leaped up inside her. But his hand stayed at his side, and he turned his gaze back to the screen.

She moved her hand toward him, and then pulled it back.

After the movie they went to Pizza and Brew next to the theater. Waiting for their pizza, Laura looked around the crowded restaurant.

"Do you know any of these people?" Laura asked Paul. "I don't see anyone from Edgemont. Are they from Woodlands?"

"Some of them look familiar. But I don't know that many people yet. I think the jocks are here, and I don't know any of them."

"You're not into sports?"

"Not exactly," he said, smiling at her. "My sport is getting out of bed, at least once a day, and tying my own shoelaces, and—let's see—walking Folly every morning before school."

Laura laughed. "That's it? Don't you have to take phys ed at school?"

"Yeah, but I don't go out for any of the teams—if that's what you mean. Back in New York I was on the chess team and I wrote for the school newspaper. But it's hard to do that here when everyone's known each other for years and years. That's one reason I like working at Harmony House. They just started having high-school kids volunteering there, so I don't feel like—well—like the new kid on the block."

"Well, I think you're wonderful to be working there. It makes me feel guilty. All I do after school is homework."

"Don't forget you have a very important job, too. Walking Folly."

Laura laughed. "Oh, sure. But how is he doing?"

"Not so good. We're taking him back to the vet again."

"How's your father? He wasn't feeling so well about a week ago."

"He's a little better, I guess. It's hard to tell with him."

The waitress arrived with their pizza, and they each pulled off a slice and put it on their plates. The melted cheese and the spicy aroma of the tomato sauce was too wonderful for Laura to resist.

"Ow!" she wailed.

"What's the matter?"

"I burned my mouth. I always do that. You'd better wait."

Paul touched his slice of pizza. "Ouch! Thanks for warning me. By the way, how's your mom doing?"

This was the time to tell him the truth. Yes, she'd do it. But, instead, she heard herself say, "She's doing okay." She couldn't say the words *cancer—mastectomy—breast*. And now there was another word: *nodes*. Her mother had one positive node, something that the doctor took out from under her arm to see if the cancer had spread. Positive meant bad, and negative meant good. It was all crazy. But having one positive node was better than having three or four—or more—her mother had told her. It meant they had caught the cancer at a fairly early stage, so maybe everything would be all right.

She looked at Paul eating his slice of pizza. If she told him the truth, of course he'd be sympathetic. But maybe he'd wonder if it was going to happen to Laura, too.

She reached for another slice of pizza. "This is really good. I was starving."

"Me, too. What else should we have? Want some ice cream?"

"Ice cream? Great!" That's what she wanted. Something cold and sweet and smooth. Something that would relieve the hot, anxious feeling filling her chest, her throat, her head.

"What kind? You want a sundae?"

"Yeah. A hot fudge sundae." She looked at her watch. "Listen, will you order it while I call my father? I told him we wouldn't stay out too late."

While she dialed her number at the rear of the restaurant, she thought of asking her father not to say anything to Paul about her mother's surgery. But that was silly. Her father was the last person in the world to talk about it. She'd be surprised if he said much more to them than "How was the movie?"

"Hi, Dad. Did I wake you?"

"No, I'm up."

She could see him stretched out on the big bed, fully dressed, her mother probably asleep beside him. Usually the two of them read in bed together before going to sleep.

"Can you come for us in half an hour? We're at the pizza place next to the movie theater. You know where I mean?"

"Yes, I know. I'll leave in a little while."

They stood outside, looking at the steady progression of headlights moving toward them.

"So—what kind of car do you have?" Paul asked.

"A white Toyota. So—" she said, and smiled.

"So?" He smiled back at her.

"So—you're going to be sixteen on Friday. Are you celebrating?"

"Yeah. My parents are taking me out for dinner. Want to come with us?"

"Oh, hey, I didn't mean to—I mean—that must have sounded like I was fishing for an invitation."

"No, it didn't. As a matter of fact, I was thinking of asking you."

"You were? Really? Like when?"

"Like just a minute ago. See—you really are psychic. You were getting my thought waves."

"But what about your parents? Shouldn't you ask them first?"

"Listen, my father is already crazy about you, don't ask

me why." He grinned at her. "And my mother really likes you, too. So I know they'll say yes."

"Well then," she said, smiling, "I'd love to. Thanks."

"Good. Do you like Italian food—besides pizza?"

"I love it."

A car honked and a pair of headlights drew up close to them.

"That's my dad," Laura said.

They got into the backseat. "Dad, this is Paul."

"Hi," her father said.

No one spoke while they drove out of the parking lot. A few blocks later, her father turned to them.

"How was the movie?" he asked.

Laura and Rachel had been to six different stores in the Galleria shopping mall.

"I still think you'll be safest with a CD," Rachel said as they walked through the crowded arcade.

"I don't want to be safe," Laura said. "Everyone gives that. I want to be original. And besides, I don't know what he likes or has."

They continued walking.

Rachel was looking in a luggage store window. "What about one of those wallets?"

"I was thinking of that, too—but that's not very original, either."

"Laura! You're going to drive me crazy. If you want to be original, why don't you make him something?"

"Come on, Rache, his birthday's tomorrow. What can I make him? An ashtray out of Play-Doh?"

"That's an idea," Rachel said, laughing. "Does he smoke?"

"No, he doesn't. Seriously—what would he like that won't seem dumb or tacky or too personal?"

"I don't know. I think all the other things you almost bought were fine. A book was a good idea."

"But I don't know what he likes to read."

"That's the trouble, if you ask me. You hardly know him."

"I know about the important things. I just don't know the little details."

"Okay. My last suggestion. Give him something to eat. Everyone likes that. Buy him some candy, or—"

"Hey, I'll bake him some cookies. That's what I'll do. Terrific! Thanks, Rache." She gave Rachel a hug. "You're a genius!"

"Sure, sure," Rachel said, smiling. "And you're insane. Now can we shop for ourselves?"

Laura made a double batch of chocolate chip cookies, knowing that she would have to give some of them to her family. Charlie stood next to her as she lifted the cookies off the baking sheets and piled them onto a couple of plates. Two hands reached out toward the plates.

"Hey, take your grubby paws away from my cookies," Laura said sharply. "I'll give you two—and that's all! And I'm trusting you," she added. She put three cookies on a small dish and started out of the kitchen.

"Who are those for?" Charlie asked.

"Mom."

Her mother was sitting in her bedroom in her pale green bathrobe, talking on the phone.

"That's just the way it feels. I'm glad to hear that it doesn't last," her mother was saying. "Listen, Laura has just arrived with some delicious-looking cookies, so I'll speak to you tomorrow—okay?" She put down the phone and turned to Laura.

"Hello, my love. Don't they look good. Did you make them?"

"Yes. They're fresh out of the oven. Who was that? Ruth?"

Her mother nodded and took one of the cookies. "Mmm. These are delicious. What, may I ask, has prompted this bit of domesticity?"

"It's Paul's birthday tomorrow, and I couldn't think of a good present to buy, so I decided to bake him some cookies."

"Paul—the Rosens' son?"

"Right. The whole family is really wonderful—and Paul invited me to go out to dinner with him and his parents tomorrow night. Okay?"

Her mother smiled. "Okay."

"Anyway, I was wondering if you have some kind of box I could put the cookies in."

"I think I do. I keep a bunch of gift boxes in the closet in the den. I think Dad's there now. Maybe you can spare a couple of cookies for him. He could use a little cheering up."

"For me?" Her father looked up from his desk. A half-finished crossword puzzle was in front of him. "Hey, thanks, pal. They look good," he said, and took one of the cookies. "They *are* good."

Laura stood beside him as he put the puzzle aside to take up a pile of bills. She took a deep breath. Now was her chance.

"Dad?" she said quietly.

He looked up. "What's up?" her father said. "Something on your mind?"

"Mom showed me the poem you wrote for her."

Her father raised his eyebrows. "Really?"

Laura nodded. "I really liked it. I wish . . . I wish I could see more."

"That's quite a compliment." Her father smiled. "Maybe when things calm down around here, there'll be time for that."

"It's been hard lately, with Mom sick," Laura said.

Her father turned back to his bills, while Laura's mind filled with questions.

"So," Laura started, "how is Mom really doing, Dad? Is there a chance her cancer might spread and she might . . . might . . ." She couldn't say the word.

Her father hesitated. "I'm not a doctor, honey. I just don't know."

She waited for more, but he had pulled out his check-book and was already busy writing.

She went into the closet and found a white box that looked about the right size. On the lid there was a long single red rose. The rose was a nice touch.

As she came out of the closet, her father said, "You left the light on in the closet."

She switched off the light.

Wasn't there something else he could say to her? Isidor would have said something funny, knowing she needed cheering up, too.

Back in the kitchen, lining the box with aluminum foil and carefully filling it with the cookies, she thought of her father sitting quietly at his desk, paying the bills, paying for all the things they spent money on—her new clothes, music lessons, camp, and summer vacations. But she remembered the letters he wrote her when she went to camp each summer. They were sweet letters. They even had jokes in them. And sometimes funny drawings. Her father was a different person in his letters.

chapter twelve

Everything on the menu looked expensive, and it was all written in Italian. Please, Laura prayed silently to the waiter who was standing by their table. Don't ask me first.

"I'm going to have the braciola," Isidor said.

"Isidor—no red meat. Remember?" Miriam said.

"It won't be red when it gets here. Nobody makes braciola rare."

"That's not the point. No beef. That's what Dr. Hoffman said."

"Dr. Killjoy." Isidor sighed, and looked at his menu again.

"I'll have the filet of sole Florentine," Miriam said. "What about you, Laura? What would you like?"

"Gee, uh—I'm afraid my Italian is a little rusty," Laura said, hoping she would sound witty, "so I'm not sure what most of this means."

"Listen, dear wife," Isidor said. "Do I have your permission to have the chicken Marsala?"

"Yes, dear husband, you do. And don't look so deprived. I'm sure it'll be delicious."

"I think I'll have the same," Laura said. She didn't know what it was, but it sounded like a safe choice.

"Me, too," Paul said. "The same. I have a feeling I shouldn't have eaten so many of those cookies."

In the car, on the way to the restaurant, Paul had opened the box of cookies and after giving one to each of them, had kept on eating them.

"That's right," Isidor said. "You shouldn't have. Now there won't be enough left for me. Who taught you to make such delicious cookies, Laura?"

"My mother."

"Paul, you should have invited her mother to this birthday party, too."

"Her mother's just home from the hospital," Miriam said. She turned to Laura. "How's she doing?"

So Paul had told her.

"She's okay," Laura said. "She just gets tired pretty quickly." Please. No more questions.

The waiter returned with their orders and they started to eat.

"What else does your mother do—besides bake?" Isidor asked.

"She teaches English at the community college," Laura said.

"I guess she's taking some time off to recover," Miriam said.

"Yes," Laura said. "She's taking the rest of the semester off. She says she's going to catch up on her reading and listen to lots of music."

"Does your mother play an instrument?" Isidor asked.

"She plays the piano a little bit. But my brother is the one who's really good at the piano. In fact, he's amazingly good."

"And what about you? When am I going to hear you play that flute of yours?"

"Oh, you wouldn't want to hear that. I told you—I play it really badly."

"Never mind 'badly.' You bring it over, and I'll accompany you on the piano, and then you'll know what 'badly' means. How about coming over on Sunday?"

Laura looked at Paul. She didn't know what to say.

"Come in the afternoon," Miriam said. "We'll have tea. Maybe there'll be some of your cookies left."

"Don't count on it," Paul said. "But come and bring your recipe and we can make some more."

The three of them all smiled expectantly at her. "Thanks," she said. "I'd love to come."

"Good, and now that that's all settled," Isidor said, "let's address the question that even the Supreme Court has been unable to answer. Do you know what that is, dear friends?"

"Don't answer him," Miriam said.

"Okay, Dad," Paul said, pretending to be annoyed. "What is it?"

"No one knows? All right, I'll tell you. The question is, What shall we have for dessert?"

"I told you not to answer him," Miriam said.

"Never mind her," Isidor said. "These are your choices." And then he began to sing.

"Spumoni or tortoni,
Tortoni or spumoni.
Or maybe cannelloni,
Or a chocolate ice-cream coney."

Laura and Paul laughed. Miriam laughed, too, and said, "Isidor, you need a new song. That one's a hundred years old."

"Good," Isidor said. "That makes it an antique. Maybe I can sell it."

The waiter arrived carrying a small chocolate cake with a candle in the center. Two other waiters came with him, and they started singing "Happy Birthday" to Paul. Miriam and Isidor and Laura joined in. Paul grinned happily at all of them.

On Saturday afternoon Laura came into the kitchen and found her mother and Ruth sitting at the table, slowly turning the pages of a book.

"What're you looking at?" Laura asked, opening the refrigerator.

"I brought your mother a book about breast reconstruction," Ruth said. "Want to see?" Laura grimaced and Ruth quickly added, "No, I can see you don't."

"Do you think you'll do it, Mom?" Laura asked.

"I don't know," her mother said. "You hear so many different things about which way is the safest. I want Ruth to try it first, and she wants me to."

"I told your mother we should do it together. We can be roommates in the hospital."

Laura wondered how they could talk about it so lightly.

Laura sat at her desk, trying to study for Monday's French test, but her mind kept drifting back to the Rosens' invitation for Sunday afternoon. Paul said she should bring the cookie recipe. She'd better go downstairs and get it.

From the living room she heard a woman's voice singing in German. It was one of the CDs her mother liked so much.

The music was beautiful, and she paused in the doorway to listen. Her parents were sitting on the couch reading.

This was Isidor's kind of music, she thought. In the Rosens' living room right now, they were probably all joking or talking or teasing one another.

Her mother suddenly put her book down and burst into tears.

"Annie, what's the matter?" her father asked.

Her mother didn't answer. Her shoulders shook as she sobbed, her hands covering her face.

Laura knelt down in front of her. "Mom, what is it?"

Her mother shook her head, and took out a crumpled tissue from her pocket. She wiped her face and blew her nose.

"I'm sorry," she murmured. "That song—it's so beautiful—it just undoes me."

"Should I turn it off?" Laura asked.

"Yes. No, leave it on. It's almost at the end."

"Why that song, Mom?"

"It's Schubert's 'Spring Dreams,' and it's about being young and beautiful and being in love—and then it's all over."

Her father pulled her close. "Annie, you mustn't think that way. It's not all over."

Her mother didn't answer.

The music ended, and Laura left her parents sitting on the couch together holding hands.

She found the recipe in the kitchen and was starting up the stairs, when her father came out of the living room.

"How's Mom?" Laura asked.

"Having a tough time," her father said.

"Why? Has her cancer spread?"

Her father stared at the carpet and finally sighed. "I don't think so," he said.

"Dad, talk to me," Laura said. "What's going on?"

"I don't have any more answers than you do," he said. "I wish I did, sweetie."

chapter thirteen

Sunday Laura played her flute until her lips hurt so much she had to stop.

"It was nice hearing you play your flute," her mother said at lunch. "I love that sound. What made you decide to start again?"

"Nothing special. I just thought I'd see if I still remembered how."

"Would you like me to accompany you on the piano? I think I'm up to a short piece or two."

Laura hesitated. "No. But thanks, anyway."

Her mother sighed.

"I know I'd sound terrible, Mom," Laura said. "Maybe Charlie will play some duets with you. If you want great music, he's your man."

"You sound good, too," her mother said.

"No," Laura insisted. "Not even close."

At Paul's house, they could all laugh over their mistakes. But here, her mistakes were just embarrassing.

*   *   *

After lunch, Laura put on a sweater and, with her flute case in her hand, started toward the kitchen door. Her mother was sitting at the kitchen table, the Sunday *New York Times* spread out before her. She looked up at Laura.

"I'm going over to the Rosens for a little while, Mom."

Her mother frowned. "You're going there *again*?"

"Yes. I'll be back before supper."

"I see you're bringing your flute."

"Isidor wants me to play it while he accompanies me on the piano."

As soon as the words were out, Laura wished she could take them back.

"So, you'll play with him, but not with me. I see." Her mother turned back to the newspaper on the table.

"He says I shouldn't worry about playing badly," Laura said. "He says he plays badly, too." She hoped that would make her mother feel a little less hurt.

"Have a good time," her mother said in a toneless voice, keeping her eyes on the newspaper.

"Why are you being such a grouch?" Laura shouted. "Aren't I entitled to have a life?" She opened the kitchen door and slammed it shut behind her.

Walking the few blocks to Paul's house, Laura tried to forget what had just happened with her mother. It was a beautiful day, and all the Rosens wanted her to come over. That's what mattered.

The sun was shining on the few golden leaves that clung to the trees. Soon all the leaves would be gone and it would be winter, but she didn't mind. She loved the snow—and there was Hanukkah and Christmas to look forward to. She was glad her family celebrated both holidays.

Miriam opened the door for her. "Hi, Laura," she said. "Paul will be back in a few minutes. He's walking Folly."

Isidor was conducting some music in front of the stereo in the living room. It was loud and dramatic and again it sounded familiar. Miriam settled on the couch with the newspaper.

"Just in time," Isidor said as his arms continued to move rhythmically up and down. "Cellos." He nodded to the speaker on one side of the stereo. "Strings." He waved to the speaker on the other side. "Do you know what this is?" he asked Laura, still moving his arms.

"Mozart?" Laura asked timidly.

"Right," he said, his arms now still. "And I'll give you a hint. It's about a man who was probably the most charming no-goodnick in history. At least literary history."

"Oh, now I remember. That's my father's favorite opera. *Don Giovanni.*"

"Ah, I see your father is man of exquisite taste. Is that why your mother married him?"

"I doubt it. Her favorite opera is *The Marriage of Figaro.*"

"A *woman* of exquisite taste. I married Miriam because she could play the cello. It's awfully hard to find a cellist these days."

"Isidor!" Miriam cried. "What kind of nonsense are you telling this poor girl? Laura, I've never played the cello."

"I only said you *could* play the cello, if it were necessary."

Laura and Miriam both laughed. "Isidor, that's why *I* married you—because you're so crazy."

The front door opened and Paul came into the room. Folly appeared behind him, moving more slowly than ever.

He greeted Laura with a few friendly sniffs, his long, feathery tail swaying weakly back and forth.

"Hello, Folly." Laura bent down to stroke him. "How's my friend?"

Folly looked back at her with his big dark eyes.

"Mom," Paul said, "he's really bad. He kept lying down. I had to pull him most of the way back."

"Oh, dear," Miriam said. "I'll call Dr. Berman first thing in the morning."

Folly lay down on the floor and closed his eyes.

"Maybe he'll feel better after he has a nap," Miriam said.

"Are you going to make cookies with me?" Paul asked Laura. "The ones you gave me are almost gone."

"Listen—I need Laura for just five minutes," Isidor said. "I want to play the overture for her and then you can have her—for a while."

"What do you mean 'for a while'?" Paul asked.

"She's finally brought her flute, so when your cookies are in the oven, Laura and I are going to make hideous music together."

"Hideous is right." Laura laughed. "And you'll be sorry."

"All right—five minutes," Paul said. "I'll turn on the oven and get started."

"I'll help you." Miriam followed Paul into the kitchen.

Isidor switched the stereo back on. "I want you to hear this from the beginning," he said. "It's the overture, and it's in D minor, a key that has special meaning for Mozart. Listen."

Laura sat in the large chair opposite the couch and heard the familiar progression of dark, ominous chords.

"That's the sound of the avenging fate that will overtake Don Giovanni. We'll hear these chords again in the last act. Now listen to these scales—still in D minor."

As the music rose solemnly up the scale, Isidor slowly raised his arms above his shoulders. But then, just as the music started down the scale, Laura heard a wheezing sound. She looked down at Folly. His chest was moving slowly up and down and now he was taking loud, rasping breaths.

Isidor switched off the stereo and kneeled by Folly's side, gently stroking the dog's head. "Hey, old boy, what's the matter?" The labored breathing continued. "Laura, you'd better get Miriam and Paul."

Laura ran to the kitchen. "Something's wrong with Folly!"

The car moved quickly through the sparse Sunday traffic. Paul and Laura sat in the backseat with Folly wrapped in an old blanket. His head was on Paul's lap, and Paul kept stroking him. Folly looked up at him with dark, trusting eyes. His breathing was heavy and slow.

"How is he?" Miriam asked from the front seat.

"The same," Paul said.

"We're almost there," Miriam said.

Suddenly a tremor shook Folly's body. He heaved a deep shuddering gasp, and then he was still.

Laura held her breath. Folly stayed silent, his open eyes staring blankly at nothing.

"Mom!" Paul cried out in a strangled voice.

"What? What's the matter?"

"I think he's dead."

"Oh no," Miriam said. Pulling the car over to the side of the road, she leaned over her seat and stroked Folly's head. Then she laid her hand on Folly's side.

"Paul, I'm so sorry."

Paul stared out the window.

"I guess we'll keep going," Miriam said after a few moments. "Dr. Berman will know what to do."

At the parking lot Miriam told them to wait in the car while she went into the office. Laura could see that Paul was trying not to cry. Folly's body rested warm and heavy on their laps.

When Miriam returned with a young man in a white uniform, there were tears in her eyes. The man lifted Folly gently out of the car. Miriam followed him back to the office.

Laura and Paul got out and stood next to the car. The sky had become overcast, and a cold wind blew some scattered leaves about their feet. Laura hugged herself, wishing she had worn a warm jacket instead of just a sweater. Paul's eyes were on the door to the vet's office.

She put her hand on his shoulder. "He was such a great dog," she said softly. There was a lump in her throat.

Paul leaned on the hood of the car and started to sob.

When Paul finally turned to face her, his eyes were red and his dark hair had fallen forward over his forehead. Laura reached out to him and held him close. He put his arms around her and rested his head on her shoulder.

Isidor was stretched out on the couch with his eyes closed.

"Is he all right?" Paul asked with a worried look.

"Yes," Miriam said. "He's just sleeping. He must have been tired."

"I'll walk you home," Paul said to Laura.

"I can't believe it," Paul said as they walked slowly toward her house. "I've had Folly for so long—almost half my life. I can't believe I'll never see him again."

"I know," Laura said. "I can't believe it, either." She took a deep breath. "Paul—I've been wanting to tell you something, and this is probably a dumb time to tell you—"

"Tell me what?"

"About my mother. I didn't tell you the truth—about her operation."

Keep going now. Don't stop.

"She has cancer." Go all the way. "She had a mastectomy."

A car went past, sending up a flurry of leaves in its wake.

"That's lousy," Paul said. "That's really lousy."

"Yeah. It is."

"Why didn't you want to tell me before?"

"I don't know. It was just so hard to talk about. I mean—it's hard to even think about."

They walked along in silence until they stood together in Laura's driveway.

"Listen—" Paul said at last. "I'm glad you told me about your mother." He reached for her hands. "You should have told me before. I mean—I'm your friend."

"I know," she said.

He looked at her sadly. "I'd better go," he said. "I'm kind of worried about my father."

"I'm so sorry about Folly, Paul." Tears brimmed in Laura's eyes. "If you need to talk—"

"I know. I'll call you," he said.

"Right." She hugged him and then went inside just before the tears rolled down her face.

chapter fourteen

"I'm exhausted." Her mother threw her coat on the kitchen chair. She was just back from a doctor's appointment in New York.

"What did the doctor say?" Laura asked.

"I'll tell you in a minute, but let me first put on some water for tea."

"I'll do it," Laura said. "You sit down and tell me."

Her mother sat down at the table. "I don't know why I was so surprised, but with only one positive node, I thought Dr. Gordon would say I wouldn't need any chemotherapy. Unfortunately, he didn't."

"Chemotherapy? What does it do to you?"

"That's what I asked him—plus a million other questions. He was really very nice about it—he gave me a lot of time. He said it wasn't as bad an ordeal as people expect, but I might lose my hair."

"Lose your *hair*?"

"Yes, sometimes that happens. But not to everyone—and he said it's only temporary. Your hair grows back."

The kettle started to boil and Laura got out a cup and saucer. Her mother without hair! That would be worse than losing a breast. Everyone would see.

"Of course if that happened," her mother continued, "I'd get a wig. But maybe this time I'll be lucky."

"I hope so, Mom." Laura took the kettle off the stove. "What kind of tea do you want?"

"Something nice. How about Lemon Lift. Maybe it'll lift my spirits. You going to have some?"

Laura hesitated. She longed to be up in her room, to forget about what her mother had told her. "Sure," she said. "I'll have some Lemon Lift, too."

At dinner that night her mother explained to her father and Charlie what the doctor had said about her having chemotherapy. Injections and pills—with weird sounding names—all going into her mother's body. Two weeks on them and then two weeks off.

Laura tuned it all out until she heard Charlie say, "But it's not my turn. It's Laura's turn."

"My turn for what?" Laura asked.

"To load the dishwasher," Charlie said.

"It's not my turn. I did it yesterday. And I set the table tonight."

"So what," Charlie said. "I've been clearing off."

"Big deal," Laura said. "I'll finish clearing for you, but it's not my turn to load. I've got a biology test tomorrow."

"You always have a test. It wouldn't kill you to load the

dishwasher. Setting the table is nothing, and I already did most of the clearing, so—"

"Stop it!" her mother suddenly shouted. "I can't stand it!"

"But, Mom—it's not fair," Charlie said. "Laura's always—"

"Stop it!" Her mother shouted again, this time more loudly. "Stop it! Stop it! Stop it!"

Everyone looked at her.

"I can't believe I'm hearing this." Her mother's voice was icy. "Doesn't this mean anything to you? Doesn't anything register on your self-centered little minds? Does life just go on as though nothing has happened?"

Laura and Charlie stared at the table. Finally their father said, "I'll load the dishwasher. You two should be ashamed of yourselves."

"I'll do it," Laura said.

"I'll do it," Charlie said, "after I finish clearing."

Her mother pushed back her chair. "Do it or don't do it," she said. "You can throw the dishes in the garbage. I don't care what you do." She turned and left the dining room, her footsteps pounding up the stairs.

"Laura. Telephone," her father called from her parents' bedroom later that night.

"I'll take it downstairs," she called back.

She went to the kitchen and picked up the phone. "I've got it," she said, and waited for the click of her father hanging up before saying hello.

"Hi. It's me. Paul."

"Hi. I was going to call you. You must feel so terrible about Folly."

"I do. And I just had a fight with my parents about him.

I wanted them to get him back from the vet so we could bury him."

"Where?"

"Well, at first I said in our backyard. But it turns out we're not allowed to do that. Then I wanted to have him buried at that pet cemetery on Central Avenue, but they said no."

"Why? Too expensive?"

"How'd you guess? It costs at least three hundred and fifty dollars—plus extra to take care of the plot. I told them I'd pay for it, but they said that was silly. It wouldn't make sense even if it didn't cost so much because they don't know how long we'll be living here."

Laura caught her breath. Finally she said, "Didn't you just move here?"

"Yeah—in September. So that really got me mad. I mean, they don't know what it's like to change schools in the middle of high school—to have to make new friends—to finally meet someone—people—you like—"

"Are they planning to move again soon?"

"No. They said if all goes well, we would stay here at least until I finish high school."

"What do they mean—'if all goes well'?" Laura asked.

"If all goes well with my father. I think they're planning eventually to move someplace warmer. The cold weather is hard on him. But I wasn't in the mood to talk about it, and I guess they weren't either."

"Listen—what are you doing Saturday?"

"Nothing. What are you doing Saturday?"

"Something with you. You need to be cheered up. How about we take our bikes and have a picnic somewhere?"

"What if it rains?"

"It won't."

"Or snows—"

"Hey, you're really in bad shape. It's a good thing you called me."

Laura and Rachel sat together in the school library during their Friday morning study period.

"How's your mom doing?" Rachel whispered.

"She's going to have chemotherapy," Laura whispered back.

"Oh no. Really?"

"Yeah. She saw two doctors this week, and they both told her she should. I don't think I could stand it if she loses her hair." Laura was silent for a moment. "Oh, Rache, I can't believe I said that. It sounded terrible. Of course, it would be worse for her—but just thinking about it gives me the creeps. Do you know anyone who's had chemotherapy?"

"My uncle. He had Hodgkin's disease, and he's fine now."

"Did he lose his hair?"

"I don't know. He was practically bald before he got sick."

Laura felt a hand on her shoulder.

"Please, girls, be quiet." It was Mrs. Lewis, the librarian. "I don't usually have to remind you two."

"Sorry," Laura said softly. Mrs. Lewis moved away and Laura was glad to have an excuse to stop talking about her mother.

Rachel opened her notebook and wrote on a sheet of paper: *How are things with you and Paul?*

Laura took Rachel's pen and wrote back: *Good, I think. I'm seeing him on Saturday.*

Lucky, Rachel wrote: *Does he have a friend?*

Laura saw that Rachel was blushing. *I don't know. I'll ask him.*

chapter fifteen

She was ahead of Paul as they rode up the hill. At the entrance to the park she got off her bike and waited.

"Slowpoke," she said, smiling at him when he caught up to her, all out of breath. "You're really out of shape."

"I know," he said. "What's your secret?" He laid his bike on the grass and sat down beside it.

"Practice. Experience." She sat down beside him.

"Oh, you're experienced, are you?"

"At bike riding, yes."

"That's all?"

"What do you think?"

"I don't know. Girls are a mystery to me."

"I'm not 'girls.' I'm me. Am I a mystery to you?"

He looked at her a moment. "I guess you are, in some ways. Am I a mystery to you?"

She thought of his unfinished letter, his shyness. "Yeah, I guess you are, too."

Both of them laughed.

"So what do we do now?" he asked. "You said you've been here before."

"When I was a Girl Scout, we used to have our picnics here. You need a permit to use the place in the summer, but now we'll probably have it all to ourselves."

They wheeled their bikes through the entrance and rode along a narrow paved path that wound through the park. The ground was mostly covered with leaves, but here and there patches of grass showed through.

"How about over there?" Laura pointed to a grassy area near a large tree.

"Okay," Paul called back.

Laura spread out the old blanket she had brought.

"That was smart—bringing a blanket," he said. "Why didn't I think of that?"

"I don't know. Why didn't you?"

"I guess I was busy thinking about what I would eat— not about what I would sit on."

"So, what did you bring?"

"Two meat loaf sandwiches. My mother makes great meat loaf. You're welcome to have some. And a Coke. What did you bring?"

Laura opened her bag and started to take things out. "Let's see. An egg salad sandwich, a Sprite, and a bag of Pepperidge Farm fruit cookies. They're for both of us."

"Good. Let's eat," he said. "I'm starving."

Paul finished his first sandwich and was reaching into his bag for the second one. Laura glanced across the blanket at him. There was fringe of soft dark hairs above his mouth. His brown eyes were warm, shy.

"What're you looking at?" he asked.

"You, I guess."

"Oh. What do you see?" He took a bite of his sandwich.

"I see ketchup on your mouth."

He wiped his mouth with the back of his hand. "Gone?"

Laura nodded.

"Want some of this?" He broke his sandwich in half.

"Okay. Thanks." Laura took a bite of the sandwich.

"Now you've got ketchup on *your* mouth," he said.

She reached into her bag for a paper napkin and wiped her mouth. "Is it off?"

"I can't really tell," he said. He moved closer to her.

"Well?"

"I still don't know. I'll have to get closer." He put his hands on her shoulders. "There's only one way to be really sure."

"What's that?"

"Close your eyes."

She closed her eyes, and then, at last—at last—he kissed her. She leaned toward him. His lips were warm and soft. When he pulled away, she opened her eyes. His eyes were open, too. They smiled at each other.

"Ketchup all gone?" she asked.

"I'm afraid so."

A strong breeze scattered the papers from their lunch. They gathered them up and stuffed them back into their bags. Just as they started walking back to their bikes, a large black dog came sauntering down the path near their tree. He paused to look at them and then kept on going.

"Boy, I miss Folly," Paul said.

"I miss him, too," Laura said.

"What are you doing with your extra time—now that you're not walking him anymore?"

"Oh, the usual. Homework and more homework."

"Homework? You're kidding! Why is homework so important?"

"Why? Because I take school seriously. Because I want to get good grades and get into a good college."

"You sound like my father."

"Your father? Come on."

"You don't know that side of him. You think he's all jokes and Mozart. Well, he isn't. First he wanted me to be a professional musician. Now he thinks I should be a doctor or scientist—all the things he never got to be."

"Why didn't he?"

"Well, his father died when he was still in high school. He had to help support his mother and his younger brother and sisters. He went to college at night and medical school was too expensive. Anyway, he thinks I should spend more time on homework and studying for tests so I can go to an Ivy League school. Is that what your father thinks?"

"I don't really know what my father thinks. He's never said. Whatever I do seems okay with him. I'm the one who cares about things like grades. I can't help it. It's the one thing I'm good at. Sometimes I envy the kids who go to the Alternative School."

"What's that?"

"It's a small school inside our regular high school, and the kids don't get grades there. It's very informal—they even call their teachers by their first names."

"It sounds great. Why don't you go there?"

"I guess I'm afraid I wouldn't work hard enough if I didn't know I was going to get a grade—and then maybe I wouldn't get into a really good college."

"Have you decided what you want to study when you get into that really good college?"

"No. Not really. I just know that I want to have an interesting career. What about you?"

"I haven't decided, either. But I like working with the kids at Harmony House. Maybe I'll be a psychologist. Or maybe I'll surprise my father and study medicine, after all."

"Why is that so important to him?"

"He says he's gotten bored being a pharmacist. He says I should do something that I won't get tired of."

"Listen, I have an idea. Do you think there might be a job for me at Harmony House this summer?"

"Hey, that's a great idea. I'm sure there'll be one. Maybe we could work with the same group."

The sky had become overcast, and the air began to feel chilly. But Laura didn't mind. It had been a wonderful day, and even though Paul had told her earlier that he would be in Philadelphia visiting his grandparents the whole Thanksgiving weekend, now she could look forward to being with him all summer.

"Where'd the sun go?" Paul asked. "I'm freezing."

"Me, too. Let's bike around for a while. That'll warm us up."

Their tires crunched over the crisp leaves on the path. As Paul rode ahead of her, she wondered when he'd kiss her again.

On Sunday night Laura's father came into her room and asked to borrow some of her bubble bath crystals.

"I didn't know you like bubble baths," she said. "Is that what the new men are into these days?"

She thought he'd smile at that, but he didn't. Instead, he looked upset, and avoided meeting her eyes.

"They're for Mom. Tonight she's allowed her first bath, and I thought some bubbles might make it a little easier."

Then she understood the look on his face.

"Oh. Has she—has she taken the bandages off yet?"

"No. She's going to do it in a few minutes. I offered to be with her, but she says she wants to do it alone."

Laura listened for water running in her parents' bathroom. Then she went into the den to watch a short program on the Constitution that her social studies teacher had assigned. When it was over she went back upstairs. Everything was quiet.

Just as she reached the door, her father came out of the master bedroom with the bottle of bath crystals in his hand.

"Thanks, babe," he said.

As she took the bottle, Laura couldn't stop herself from imagining her mother's scars and the empty place.

"Has Mom gone to bed?"

"No. She's taking a long soak. I'm sure she'd like to see you before she goes to bed."

Laura bit her lip. "I'm pretty tired, Dad. But, tell her good night. I'll see her in the morning."

"Okay. I'll tell her."

In bed, lying in the dark, Laura imagined her mother looking up at the ceiling as the bubbles covering her slowly disappeared. She saw her getting out of the tub, drying off, looking at herself.

Laura sighed. She should have waited to say good night.

chapter sixteen

Laura leaned against her locker and closed her eyes.

It was the Monday after Thanksgiving, and she and Paul hadn't seen each other for a long time. All weekend she had been wishing she were with him in Philadelphia. Her own family had been invited to Ruth Fisher's house for Thanksgiving dinner, but she and Charlie were the only young people there, so it hadn't been much fun.

"Hey, Laura, are you asleep?" It was Rachel.

"No, I'm just resting my tired old eyes before going to gym." Laura yawned.

"What're you tired from? You just had a four-day vacation."

"Please. Some vacation. Stuck in the house with nothing to do. Anyway, I was up late last night with my history paper. How's yours coming along?"

"It isn't. I thought I'd start it when I was in Boston, but I never got to it."

"How was Boston?" Laura asked. "Did you have a good time?"

"It wasn't so great," Rachel said. "My parents were busy at their meetings, so I was on my own most of the time."

They pushed through the double doors leading to the gyms.

"So was I, unless you count Charlie."

"What about Paul—" Rachel stopped in mid-sentence. "Oh, I forgot, he was away. So I guess you haven't had a chance to ask him about double dating."

"Oh, Rachel, I'm sorry. I was going to ask Paul about a friend—I really was—but, well, I just forgot."

"That's okay. I shouldn't have said anything."

"It's not okay. I'm going to ask him the very next time I see him. Really. It would be fun—four of us going out together. Of course, I can't promise anything. Paul's new in his school, and I don't think he's gotten to know too many guys yet, but I'll ask him."

"Okay. But, listen—don't make it sound like I'm desperate."

"Of course I won't."

"I mean, I *am* desperate," she said, smiling, "but that's only for you to know."

Laura closed her notebook and got up from her desk. Her history paper wasn't going well. She kept typing words and deleting them. She went over to her stereo and put in a CD, then she turned it off.

She went into the hall. Her parents' door was partly closed. Her mother was probably in bed already. Since she had started her chemotherapy treatments, she was tired a lot of the time and went to bed early. That was all Laura knew about what the treatments did.

When Charlie started asking their mother questions about the injections the doctor gave her and the pills she took each day, Laura always tried not to listen.

She went downstairs and phoned Paul.

"Hello." An unfamiliar voice answered in almost a whisper.

"Hi. I think I might have dialed wrong. Uh—is this the Rosens?"

"Yes. Hello, Laura. This is Isidor."

"Oh, hi. It didn't sound like you. Are you all right?"

There was a pause before Isidor answered. "For an old man, I guess I'm all right. I imagine you want to speak to Paul. I'll go find him."

That was Isidor? He sounded so serious.

"Hi," Paul said. "I was going to call you." His voice sounded flat and tired.

"Hey, are you okay? I mean, you don't sound so good. And your father didn't sound right, either. What's the matter?"

"Well, my father had a bad weekend. The doctor wants him to stay home for a couple of weeks."

"That's awful. Was it the trip?"

"Who knows? He's on some different medication now, so maybe that'll help."

"I was going to ask how your Thanksgiving was, but I guess it wasn't so good."

"No. It wasn't. How about yours?"

"It was okay." Maybe when she saw him she'd tell him about her mother's chemotherapy.

Paul didn't say anything for a moment. Finally, sounding like his old self he said, "So—?"

She pictured him smiling, and she took a deep breath. "So—did you miss me?"

"Yeah, I did. Did you miss me?"

"Desperately." She laughed.

"Yeah? Wow—no kidding!"

"Listen, I have something I want to ask you," she said, remembering her promise to Rachel.

"So ask."

"Not now. When I see you."

"Oh, okay. Want to do something Friday night?"

And what's wrong with Tuesday, Wednesday, and Thursday? "Sure. Friday's great. What do you want to do?"

"I don't know. We'll think of something."

Friday afternoon brought the first snowstorm of the season. Paul called and suggested they take a walk after dinner.

The branches of the trees were heavy with fresh snow as Laura walked along the newly plowed streets. They had decided to meet at Magnolia Street because it was midway between their two houses.

Paul was waiting for her at the corner wearing a dark knitted cap and a long scarf with brightly colored stripes. He chucked a snowball at her. It landed at her feet.

"Ha, ha, you missed." She scooped up some snow and threw one back at him. He ducked.

"Truce," he said. "We're both lousy shots."

He reached for her hand. "How are you doing?" he asked.

"Okay. I'm glad to see you. It's been a long time."

"Two weeks—tomorrow."

"So you were counting, too." She smiled.

A cold wind dusted the trees with a fine white mist. Laura stamped her feet to warm up. "Let's walk," she said, "or we'll freeze."

"Sure."

She looked around at the lacy, snow-covered branches and breathed in the sharp, clear air. The only sound was the crunching of their boots against the hard-packed snow. Holding Paul's hand, Laura felt a sweet current of happiness flowing through her.

"So—what did you want to ask me?" Paul asked.

"You remember my telling you about Rachel—my best friend at school—"

"Yeah. What about her?"

"Well, she's really a terrific person. Very smart and pretty—and—"

"And you were wondering if I had a friend—right?"

"How did you know that?"

"Come on—with that introduction, it was either that— or you were trying to interest me in her, and—"

"And I'm not, so forget that. So—do you know some-one?"

"Well, there's a guy in my math class. He's quiet, but nice, and very smart. He's just about the only guy I've really gotten to know. I'll ask him."

"What's his name?—so I can tell Rachel. Her last name is Seymour. She lives on Endfield Road, in case he wants to call her."

"I'll tell him. His name is John. John Ferrari—like the car. Maybe we could all go to the movies tomorrow night. What do you think?"

"Sure. That sounds good."

The sky at the horizon was a dusky orange, and all around them the snow radiated a soft white light. It seemed as though they were walking in a magical world.

"Folly used to love the snow," Paul said. "You know—I still look for him in the morning when I wake up. How about you? Do you miss walking him?"

"Yes, I really do." And then, without thinking, she said, "He loved you a lot, too. A couple of times when I came over to walk him, I found him in your room."

"In my room? You were in my room?"

"Only to find Folly," she lied. "What's the big deal?"

"I have personal things in there," he said, and then shrugged. "I guess I can tell you. I wrote you a few letters. I kept them in a notebook in my room."

Laura swallowed, then said quietly, "I saw your notebook on your desk."

"What?"

Paul folded his arms and glared at her.

"The first time there was just a piece of paper with 'Dear Laura' written on it."

"Was there a second time, too?"

She hesitated, thinking she could say Folly was there again, and it wouldn't sound so bad. But she didn't want to lie to him anymore. She slowly nodded.

"I went in again on purpose, hoping that maybe you had written me a real letter—and that I'd find out what you really thought about me."

"That's great," he said. "Just great! Would you like to hear what I think of you now?"

"No." She looked down at the ground and kicked a clump of snow with her foot. "I know it was wrong and I'm sorry. I'm really sorry, Paul. And I never did it again. Honestly."

She wanted to look at his face to see how angry he was, but she was afraid if she did, he'd say more than she wanted to hear. Finally, she couldn't bear his silence any longer.

"What are you thinking about?" she asked.

"I'm thinking about the other letters I wrote you. Those were really interesting letters."

"And you didn't even send them to me?"

Paul shrugged. "I was thinking about mailing them."

"I'll bet. Listen. I promise from now on I'll wait for you to mail your letters before I read them. Deal?"

Paul looked at her with serious eyes. "No more snooping for top secret materials?"

"No more. Do you forgive me? Say yes. Please, Paul. I really am sorry."

"Okay. Yes." He smiled then and kissed her. She put her arms around his neck and he slid his arms down to her waist and held her.

The sound of an approaching car made them draw apart. Paul took her arm and they stepped into the snowy bank as a car with blazing headlights drove by.

"I'm getting cold," she said. "Let's go back to my house. I'll make us some hot chocolate."

Paul looked at his watch. "I'm cold, too," he said. "I'll walk you back, but then I think I'd better go home."

"So soon?" Laura asked. She stared at the ground. This wasn't much of a date. "I was really hoping to introduce you to my mother tonight."

The wind started up again. She shivered, and Paul glanced at her and then looked away.

Finally he turned to her. "I'd really like to stay out with you and go to your house. I want to meet your mother, too."

"So—why don't you?"

"Maybe it's stupid," he said, "but I just feel funny being away from home when my father's having a bad time. It's on my mind all the time."

She couldn't argue with that. "You're wonderful about your father," she said. "Much better than I am about my mother. Did I tell you that she's started her chemotherapy treatments?"

"No. How's she doing?"

"Not too bad. Mostly it makes her tired. And sometimes kind of grouchy. The chemo is the reason I wanted you to meet her tonight. Before—"

"Before what?"

Laura swallowed. "Before she loses her hair," she whispered.

Paul ran his hand through Laura's hair. "If your mother looks anything like you, she'll look terrific, with or without hair. I promise to meet her soon."

"Thank you," she said.

The lights from her house were up ahead.

"Listen," she said, "it's really cold. You don't have to walk me to the door."

"I want to walk you. And I'll call John when I get home and ask him about tomorrow night."

"If he says yes, I'll call Rachel."

"But you and I have a date, anyway. We'll go to a movie. All right?"

"All right."

They came to her driveway. He took off his mittens and stuffed them into his jacket pocket. Then, turning to her, he took her face in his hands. His fingers were warm against her cold cheeks.

"We're friends, remember?"

She nodded, and then he kissed her. A soft, sweet kiss that made her want more.

"Maybe I'll write you another letter," he said.

"Snail mail?" she asked.

"No, that takes forever. E-mail. What's your address?"

"Largo."

"Largo? How come?"

"It's got the first two letters of my first name, and the first two of my last name, and I put in the R so it would sound like a word. But also because when I played my flute, I could only play really slow pieces. So—Largo. What's your address?"

"See if you can guess. It should be easy—especially for you."

She looked at him, puzzled. And then she said, "Is it what I think it is? Folly?"

"Right," he said. "That dog is never going to be forgotten—by me, and now by you."

"I'd never forget Folly," she said. "You know that."

"Yeah, I know. Well, I'd better start back."

Laura watched the bright stripes of his scarf flapping behind him as he walked down the snow-packed street.

chapter seventeen

The movie theater had been dark and crowded, and they'd had to split up.

It was so nice holding hands with Paul that Laura had barely given a thought to how Rachel and John were getting along on the other side of the theater. After the movie they went out for pizza, and then her father picked them up. Laura hadn't been able to get Rachel alone all night, but she hoped that Rachel and John would really like each other. He certainly was great looking—and so tall and thin. But he had hardly said a word all night, at least when all four of them were together.

Now Rachel climbed into the folding cot next to Laura's bed.

"So—what do you think?" Laura asked.

"Of Paul?" Rachel said.

"No, John. We'll get to Paul later."

"I think he's nice."

"Only nice?"

"I just met him. And he's not exactly a big talker."

"Well, he just met you. He's probably a little shy."

"I don't know about that. I mean, he held my hand all through the movie. He's not shy about that. Maybe he's one of those people who doesn't like to talk."

"Maybe. But I still think it's because he's shy. Give him time. Paul was shy at first."

"And now?"

"Now—he's still shy." Laura laughed.

Rachel smiled at her. "But he's nice. I can see why you like him."

"You can? That's good. I'm glad. Don't you think John's cute?"

"Yeah, I do."

"Do you think he's someone you might really get to like?"

"I don't know what he's like under the surface. Maybe there's nothing there."

"I doubt that. Paul says he's very smart—and nice. It'll just take a little time to get to know him. It took me a while to get to know Paul—and I still don't know him that well."

They talked for a few more minutes before Rachel said, "I think I'm falling asleep."

"Me, too." Laura switched off the light on her night table. " 'Night," she said.

The room was quiet, but soon she heard her parents' voices out in the hall. Then, as she heard a door close, she tried to picture her parents together in their big bed, their bodies close together.

She wondered if they still made love. Her mother kept her door locked now when she was dressing or undressing. If they did make love, maybe it was only in the dark.

Turning onto her back, Laura reached for her breasts. Holding them, feeling their warmth and their softness, she waited for sleep.

chapter eighteen

Stop staring at him, Laura told herself. She turned her eyes away from the boy leaning over his cello in the small orchestra. Paul sat next to her in the small auditorium. Had he noticed the boy, too?

She had never seen anyone with hair so thin. It barely covered his scalp. *Cancer.* The word came to her with a stab of fear. He must have some kind of cancer and be on chemotherapy. Or maybe he was off it now and his hair was growing back. Poor kid. He was brave not to wear a wig.

She glanced at her mother sitting on the other side of her. She must have noticed him. It would be impossible not to. Laura had watched her mother every day to see if her hair was thinning. Or if it had fallen out in clumps during the night. Thank goodness, that hadn't happened.

Her mother had been smiling all evening. She'd been in a good mood for several days because this was her week off her chemo. A few days ago her mother had said that she hoped she'd never take good health for granted again.

Her father sat on the other side of her mother. Maybe he worried about her mother's hair falling out, too. And did he sometimes feel angry at her—for no reason—and then feel as guilty about it as Laura did?

Laura looked at Paul again, wishing she could talk to him. They had planned to go to a basketball game with Rachel and John tonight. Then her mother had reminded her that Charlie was playing in a concert that night at his music school.

"Invite Paul to the concert," she said. "It's about time I get to meet him."

So Laura had invited him. Actually, she was glad that Paul would hear Charlie play. Charlie's music was incredible. Maybe the next time Charlie played at a concert, she'd invite Paul's whole family to come. She knew Isidor would really be impressed.

Finally, the orchestra piece came to an end. As the audience was applauding, her mother turned to them. "Wasn't that beautiful!" she said. "Those kids are really good."

Laura nodded and turned to Paul. "My brother's next."

"I'll bet he's nervous," Paul said.

"Not Charlie. He loves performing. It's so easy for him. I'm sure glad it's not me. I hate playing in front of people."

"There are other things you're good at," Paul said.

"Like what?" Laura asked.

"Like making me smile."

Laura blushed. "Can you come back to the house later?"

Paul grinned. "See, there's the smile. Yeah, sure I can come."

The orchestra left and some men moved a large piano to the center of the stage. Soon Charlie walked down the aisle and sat down at the piano. He started to play right away, without looking at the audience. It was the Mozart sonata Laura had heard him practicing at home. It was a piece Laura really liked. Her father and her mother were smiling and holding hands as they listened.

When the piece was over, the audience applauded loudly.

"I wish I could play like that," Laura whispered to Paul. Well, she'd make her parents proud of her in a different way. This semester, the way things were going, she was pretty sure she would get A's in all her courses.

Charlie's next piece was something entirely different. It was a piece called "La Campanella," by Franz Liszt. His fingers flew over the keys, and yet Charlie looked calm. He didn't miss one note or fumble once. He raced through all those fast parts like those pianists her parents watched on TV.

When the piece was over, the audience stood up and cheered. A few people called out, "Bravo! Bravo!" Her mother and father got up, too, so Laura stood up, and then Paul did, too.

Charlie bowed several times, a big smile on his face, and then walked down the aisle and out of the auditorium. They met him in the lobby. Looking through the glass door, Laura could see that it was raining outside. Raining really hard.

"Don't kiss me," Charlie whispered to their mother.

"I wouldn't dream of it," she whispered back. And then Charlie was surrounded by a crowd of people telling him how wonderfully he played. "Like a professional," several of them said.

Laura backed away from the crowd and sighed. Even getting all A's wouldn't impress her parents—or anyone— the way Charlie's piano playing did.

"What are you doing all the way over here?" Paul asked,

joining her. "Don't you want to congratulate Charlie? He was amazing."

"Oh, he knows I'm his biggest fan," she said with a forced smile.

"I'm glad you live nearby, Paul," her father called over his shoulder as he backed out of the school parking lot. The rain was coming down in cold, gusty torrents.

"I guess you're not coming back to my house," Laura whispered to Paul.

"How would I get home?" he whispered back.

Looking out the rain-spattered window, she knew it wasn't fair to expect him to walk home in the rain, but she was still filled with disappointment.

"So, Laura," said Charlie. "You didn't say anything about the concert. Did I hurt your ears too badly? Did I strike a minor chord with you?" He laughed at his joke.

"No." Laura tried to sound enthusiastic, but her voice was flat. "You were great. Really."

"The next house on the left?" her father asked Paul.

"Yes," Paul said. "Right over there."

The car turned into Paul's driveway. An outside light was on over the front door, and down at the far end of the house, a dim light shone through closed curtains.

"Thanks for inviting me to the concert," Paul said. "I really enjoyed it." With a quick glance at Laura, he got out of the car and ran through the rain to his front door.

Laura didn't know why she was in the kitchen. She wasn't really hungry. But she wasn't sleepy, either. She opened the refrigerator, but nothing inside appealed to her. She closed it and looked at the phone on the wall.

Paul wasn't going to call. But he hadn't even said he was sorry he couldn't come back with her—or suggest they get together the next day. That was the worst part of it.

Her mother appeared in the doorway. "There you are," she said. "I was looking for you. I wanted to say good night. And to say that I liked Paul."

"I'm glad," Laura said, and then was silent.

Her mother looked at her for a moment. Then she said, "Did you notice the boy playing the cello—the one with the—"

"Yes," Laura said quickly.

"He must be on some kind of chemotherapy. I wonder if he has leukemia."

"How can he stand to look like that?"

"Maybe he's just so glad to be alive, he forgets what he looks like. He couldn't be more than fourteen or fifteen. He had such a brave-looking face."

Laura opened the refrigerator again and stared at its contents. She moved a few containers around inside, trying to look interested in the food.

"Well, I guess you don't want to talk about that."

"What's there to talk about? I don't know him—and neither do you."

"That's true. I don't. But that doesn't stop my heart from going out to him." Her mother closed the refrigerator and put her hands on Laura's shoulders. "You know, it's not a crime to have cancer. And it's not catching, either."

"I never said it was." Laura shrank away from her mother and took a step toward the doorway.

"I know you didn't. You don't say anything about it these days. As far as you're concerned, it's obviously a taboo subject."

114

"That's not true." Laura's voice rose. "That's not true at all. But that's all you talk about—cancer, cancer, cancer." Now she was shouting. "You and Ruth—you and Charlie—like there's nothing else in the world, and no one else, either. I can't stand it!"

She ran past her mother and out of the kitchen.

chapter nineteen

Laura looked out the window over her desk. It was so warm and sunny out, it was hard to believe that in two days—on Friday—it would be Christmas. The week before, her family had celebrated Hanukkah. Her parents used to give her and Charlie little presents on each of the eight nights, but now they only lit the candles on the menorah and sang some Hanukkah songs. School vacation had started the first day of Hanukkah at noon. She turned back to the list of names on her desk. She had bought gifts for everyone except Rachel.

And Paul. Maybe she shouldn't give him a present. If he didn't give her one, it would be embarrassing. Besides, she hadn't heard a word from him since the concert, but she hoped he'd want to spend lots of time with her over the vacation. She and Rachel had talked about the four of them spending New Year's Eve together.

The front door bell rang.

She went down the stairs and opened the door to find Paul standing on the front step.

"Hi," he said. "I was hoping you'd be home."

"Hi," she said. Then, looking beyond him, she saw Isidor standing at the bottom of the steps. He was bundled up in an overcoat and muffler and a red knitted hat. He waved to her. "Will you come for a short walk with old Santa Claus?"

"It's the first day warm enough for him to be outside," Paul said. "We were hoping you'd come along."

"Okay. I'll get my jacket."

She walked between the two of them down the driveway. "How are you feeling?" she asked Isidor. He looked older, smaller.

"Not bad. I'm glad to see the sun again." He gave a small smile.

"Me, too, after all that rain." They were at the street now. "Which way are you walking?"

"Back to our house," Isidor said. "That's all I'm up to today."

The afternoon sun was warm on their faces.

"Long time no see, Laura." Isidor slipped his arm in hers. "I've missed you."

"I've missed you, too." She said it automatically but then realized it was true.

"Then why didn't you stop by?" Isidor asked. "You know you're always welcome."

"I know, it's just—" She looked at Isidor's pale face, no longer full of mischievous grins and rosy cheeks. She winced at how he wheezed a little with each breath. This was what she hadn't wanted to see. "I've had a ton of homework lately."

"Those teachers need to ease up if they're keeping you so busy that you don't have time for friends," Isidor said.

"Well, now I've got two weeks of vacation," Laura said. "I'll come over and visit."

Isidor turned to Paul. "Didn't you tell her?"

Laura looked at Paul. "Tell me what?"

Paul gave her a sad look. "We're going to Boston tomorrow."

"Boston? How come?"

"They're taking me to the Lahey Clinic," Isidor said. "I'm going to be examined from my shiny bald head to my ten ugly toes—and then they'll decide."

"Decide what?"

"What to do with me. Mostly, they'll decide if I'm a good candidate for bypass surgery. A friend of mine had that a year ago, and now he plays tennis."

"Pop, you don't like tennis," Paul said.

"So? Maybe I'll start liking it."

"But why Boston?" Laura asked. "Aren't there good places in New York for that kind of thing?"

"Well, I've been to several New York doctors, and none of them seem to agree. Lahey is supposed to be the best. They have a team approach."

He stopped walking. His face was paler now, and his breathing labored.

"What's the matter, Pop?" Paul took his father's arm.

"Nothing." Isidor rolled his eyes. "Don't look so worried. I just need to rest a minute."

Soon he started walking again, and they slowly made their way to the Rosens' house. At the door Paul turned to Laura. "I'll walk you back."

"Good-bye, Laura," Isidor said. "Thanks for your company. Merry Christmas and Happy Hanukkah, and all that sort of good cheer. And speaking of cheer—try to cheer up that son of mine. He's all gloom and doom."

As Laura and Paul walked back, Paul reached for her hand. "We don't need these things, do we?" he said, and took off his gloves and then hers. His warm fingers laced with hers.

Oh, nice, she wanted to say. Nice, nice, nice. Instead she said, "How long will you be in Boston?"

"About a week. My parents have some friends there—we're going to stay with them."

"I thought you'd be around this vacation. I thought we'd have some time together."

"I thought so, too. Mom says I don't have to go with them, but I think I should."

She nodded. "Of course you should. Your folks are going to want you with them."

"I'm glad you understand," Paul said. "But I'm pretty sure I'll be back by New Year's Eve."

"I hope so. Rachel and I were thinking we'd all do something together—the four of us."

"Yeah, John told me. But he didn't say exactly what."

"We thought we'd go to a movie and then come back to my house. Rachel's parents are having a party, but mine are going out to one. And Charlie's been invited to go skiing with some friends from school. We'll have the house to ourselves."

They had reached her driveway. "Listen," she said. "I just know New Year's Eve is going to be great—so I'm crossing my fingers that you can get back."

"I'll do my best. I just never know what's going to happen."

"I know," she said, "and I'll cross my fingers that the doctors can help your father."

"Thanks. I will, too."

"I'll miss you."

"I'll miss you, too." He kissed her—a long, tender kiss. Then he started down the street.

New Year's Eve finally came. They had gone to a movie and now Paul and Rachel were cutting the pizza into slices in Laura's living room while John and Laura set up a tray of drinks in the kitchen.

"Wow!" Laura said as John poured some vodka into the pitcher of fruit punch. "I guess this is going to be a fun party."

"I sure hope so," he said. "It's time we all broke loose."

He stirred the mixture with a large spoon and tasted it. "Needs a little more," he said, and poured the rest of the bottle into the pitcher.

"Hey," Laura said. "That's a lot of vodka."

"Taste it," he said. "You can hardly tell it's there."

He was right. All she could taste was the fruit juice and just a slight taste of something bitter. "Well, as long as my parents don't find out."

"What's taking so long?" Paul called from the living room. "The pizza's getting cold."

"Be right there," John called back.

They each had a glass or two of punch with the pizza. Then they slow-danced to some of her parents' old tapes. Paul held her close as they moved slowly to the music. Rachel and John danced close together, too.

When it was almost midnight, they went into the den and turned on the TV so they could watch the New Year's Eve Ball come down in Times Square in New York. The huge crowds of people were dressed in heavy winter coats and

120

jackets. Laura felt snug and warm sitting on the couch holding hands with Paul.

She was glad John had brought the bottle of vodka. Maybe Paul would finally be less shy with her. He had had a lot more of the punch than she had, probably because he had eaten so many of those salty potato chips. Anyway, it had really helped them both relax. He told her how much he had missed her in Boston, and she told him how lonely she had been with him away. He told her how disappointed he and his parents had been when the doctors said Isidor was not a good candidate for bypass surgery. His heart was too damaged, and it would be too risky. Paul didn't know what the doctors were going to suggest instead. Maybe some new kind of medicine. His parents were staying in Boston for some additional appointments, and John was staying at Paul's house to keep him company.

"One more minute to midnight, folks," the TV announcer said.

"Hey, what about our toast?" Laura said. "Get your glasses."

She poured the last of the punch from the pitcher and they watched the ball slowly descend over the mob of people in Times Square.

"5 . . . 4 . . . 3 . . . 2 . . . 1!" a voice shouted. "Happy New Year, everyone!" A loud roar went up from the crowds, and in the background an orchestra played "Auld Lang Syne."

Laura clinked glasses with Paul.

"Happy New Year," Paul said.

"Happy New Year," she answered.

They each took a sip and kissed, a long, long kiss. When they moved apart Laura decided to ask him to come upstairs with her. And then she realized that she had to go to the bathroom.

"I'll be right back," she said. "Don't go away."

"Where would I go?" He smiled at her and leaned back against the couch cushions.

As she left the den she glanced at Rachel and John. John was kneeling in front of the TV, flipping channels. "I'm going to see if I can find some more music for dancing," he said.

"Something slow," Rachel murmured from the floor. Her eyes were closed and her head was propped up on a big throw pillow. "I'm not up to anything too energetic."

Leaving the bathroom, Laura opened her bedroom door. Her room hadn't looked so neat in years. She sprayed her neck and her hair with the cologne that Rachel had given her for Christmas. She was wearing one of her Christmas gifts from her parents—a cream-colored silky top and a new pair of jeans. Her hair was soft and shiny.

In the den she heard a band playing something nice and slow. She and Paul could dance to it, and then she would invite him up to her room.

But Paul didn't look like he was about to do any dancing. He was leaning against the cushions on the couch. His eyes were closed.

Rachel was still stretched out on the floor, her head on the big pillow, her eyes also closed.

John was kneeling in front of the cabinet where Laura's family kept their games.

"What's going on?" Laura asked.

John shrugged. He had a maroon-colored box in his hands. "Want to play Scrabble?" he said.

"Scrabble?" Laura said. "You're kidding."

"I'm not kidding. I wish I were."

"I can't believe this—and tonight of all nights."

"I know. But what can you do? So, do you like Scrabble?" He opened the box and looked around for a place to set it up. "I'll put it on the coffee table, okay?"

"Wait a minute," Laura said. "Why don't we try to wake them up."

"Be my guest. I tried with Rachel and it was hopeless. She's really out cold. Paul looks the same." John sat down on the floor in front of the coffee table and opened the Scrabble board.

Paul and Rachel were sound asleep. Paul was even snoring softly.

"I guess they're not used to drinking." She sat down on the couch opposite John. "Not that I am, either. But I didn't have so much of that punch. It must have been awfully strong."

"No, it wasn't." He picked out letters from the box and put them in his wooden letter holder. "Now you pick your letters. Seven, right?"

Laura nodded and slowly picked up the letters from the Scrabble box.

"I guess you and Rachel are in a different crowd up here," he said. "Most kids I know drink now and then—some of them a lot—so they're used to a little bit of vodka."

"It wasn't a little bit, John."

"Sure it was. You should have been in the crowd I was in back in Stuyvesant."

"Stuyvesant? That's for really smart kids, right?"

"So they say. But it doesn't stop a lot of them from doing what most kids do. The kids up here aren't so different."

"Don't you get in trouble with your parents—or don't they know?"

"Well, in the city, when my mother found out, she

grounded me for a while. My father and mother split up a few years ago, so he wasn't in the picture anymore. My stepdad is, though. He's a lawyer and has a practice in White Plains."

"That's good. He can bail you out when the police come to arrest you."

"Ha, ha. Very funny."

"Do you see much of your father?"

"No. He moved to California."

Laura looked at John's handsome, blank face. Suddenly, she didn't feel so angry with him. She couldn't imagine her father ever losing contact with her and Charlie.

"I guess it's none of my business, but why'd they split up?"

"I don't know my dad's side of it. My mom says he never really talked to her. Hey, that's what Rachel says about me, but I don't think that's true. Look—I'm talking to you, aren't I?"

Laura heard the front door opening. She looked at her watch. Her parents were home early. She went over to Paul and gently shook his shoulder. "Hey, Paul, wake up," she said.

Paul's eyes opened and he smiled at her. Then his eyes closed and he went back to sleep.

Her mother came into the living room.

Rachel opened her eyes and looked up. "Oh, hi, Mrs. Gould. Happy New Year!" Then she fell back against her pillow in a fit of giggles.

"Laura, what's going on here?" Her mother frowned.

"What do you mean? Nothing's going on." Laura couldn't look her mother in the eye. "Where's Dad?" she asked, hoping to change the subject.

"He's in the kitchen. He said he was going to take out the garbage."

"Even on New Year's Eve?"

"You know Dad. He never misses a night. Now, what's wrong with Rachel?"

Laura's father came into the living room, the empty vodka bottle in his hand.

"Where did this come from?" he asked, his voice full of angry disapproval. "It was in the trash."

Laura looked at John, who was putting away the Scrabble game. He stood up. "I'm the guilty party," he said. "I added a little to the punch."

"A little?" her mother said. Her eyes blazing, she looked at Paul and Rachel, still asleep, then took the empty bottle from her husband and held it up. "It looks like you added more than a little."

Her father took the bottle back and started to leave.

"Dan, where are you going?" Her voice was shrill. "You're her father, aren't you? Don't just run away without saying anything."

Her father turned to Laura. "Look how upset you've made your mother."

"Upset?" her mother shouted. "I'm furious! Don't I have enough problems without having to worry whether I can trust my own daughter?"

"Oh, Mom, nothing terrible happened," Laura said, "so please don't make such a big deal about it."

"Don't tell me what kind of a deal to make. Just look at your friends. Look at John, acting as though it's perfectly all right to be drinking in this house."

"But, Mom—"

"Don't 'but-Mom' me." She turned to Laura's father. "You'd better take these boys home."

Her father went over to Paul and shook his shoulder. "Paul, wake up. It's time to go home."

Paul opened his eyes and struggled to get off the couch.

Rachel sat up and rubbed her eyes.

"John, Paul," her mother said, "get your coats. My husband's taking you home. If it weren't so cold out, we'd make you walk."

Lying in her bed, with Rachel on the cot beside her, Laura wondered how she would ever fall asleep. Her very first New Year's Eve date had been ruined.

She couldn't believe her mother had talked like that in front of her friends. She was so unfair.

She looked at Rachel. There was no point in trying to talk to her. When the boys had left, Rachel had stumbled upstairs, climbed under the covers, and was immediately sound asleep with all her clothes on.

Laura looked out the window. It was such a beautiful night. There was a full moon, and that only made everything feel worse. She hoped Paul was looking at the moon, too, and thinking about her.

chapter twenty

Laura was awake by ten the next morning to say good-bye to Rachel. She would have loved some breakfast, but she was afraid her mother would be in the kitchen, and she wanted to put off facing her as long as she could. Well, she had to go to the bathroom, so she'd have to take her chances that she wouldn't run into her out in the hall.

The hall was empty, and when she left the bathroom, she heard the phone ring.

"Laura," her mother called from the kitchen. "It's for you."

She went into her parents' room. It was Paul.

"Hi," he said. "How are things in your house this morning?"

"I don't know. I'm trying to stay out of sight. What about you? Did you have any trouble when you got home?"

"Not really. My mother was asleep, but my father was up and don't ask me how, but he knew I'd had too much to drink."

"What did he say?"

"He said, 'I see you've discovered the pleasures of iniquity.' When I told him I slept through the whole thing, he said, 'I also see you've discovered those pleasures a bit too soon.'"

Laura laughed. "That's all? You were lucky."

"I know. But if my mom finds out, I may never see the light of day again. Dad won't tell, though. Listen, how'd you like to go to New York today? We could go to the Rockefeller Center market. It's fun. We could have lunch there and walk around. How does that sound?"

"That sounds great. I mean fantastic."

They both laughed.

"I'll come over around eleven thirty," he said. "Okay?"

"Sure. But, Paul, what if my mother won't let me go?"

"Don't worry. I'm going to apologize to her for last night and say that it will never happen again. Or I'll ask my father what to say. He'll think of the right words."

Laura got dressed and finally went downstairs, hoping that her mother was in a better mood and wasn't going to start in again about the night before.

Her mother was having her coffee and reading the newspaper. A glass of orange juice was at Laura's place.

"Thanks, Mom," Laura said, and drank the juice.

Her mother didn't say anything.

"I'm sorry about last night," Laura said.

Her mother looked up from her newspaper. "You should be. I don't know how you could've let John pour vodka into the punch."

Suddenly, all the disappointment from the night before came rushing back, and Laura burst into tears.

"You embarrassed me in front of my friends, Mom."

"I guess I did." Her mother's voice was softer now. "But your friends embarrassed themselves by drinking. It's over, but I hope it won't ever happen again."

"It won't, Mom. I promise."

"I accept your promise, sweetie." She leaned over and kissed Laura on her cheek. "And I didn't even get to wish you Happy New Year. I hope it's a really good year for you."

"Thanks, Mom. I hope it's a good year for you, too—and a healthy one."

There was a knock at the kitchen door. Laura got up and opened the door. It was Paul.

"Hi, Laura," he said. "Hi, Mrs. Gould. I want to apologize for last night. I'm really sorry we did something so dumb."

"Well, thank you for your apology."

He looked at Laura. She nodded encouragingly to him.

"I wanted to ask you something. Laura and I were thinking of going to New York today—to Rockefeller Center—and having lunch. Would that be all right?"

"I don't know," Laura's mother said. "I'll have to think about it."

"Oh," Paul said quickly, "my father said to wish you Happy New Year. And he made me promise we wouldn't have anything stronger than ice water."

Finally, Laura's mother laughed. "All right! All right! I can see you two are really sorry for what happened. Now go and have fun."

"I'm getting hungry," Paul said to Laura. "Where should we eat?"

They were inside the market, looking at the restaurants.

"The Swedish place is good. Let's go there," Laura said.

A waitress took them to a table in the rear and handed them menus. "You decide for me," Paul said. "Just no cabbage or eggplant."

"Okay. Let's have the cold meat smorrebrod. They're open-faced sandwiches."

"That sounds safe."

After Laura ordered for both of them, she saw Paul looking at something across the room. "What are you looking at?" she asked.

"That HAPPY NEW YEAR sign. It got me thinking about New Year's resolutions. Did you make any last night?"

For a moment she was tempted to say, No, I was too busy playing Scrabble with John, remember? But seeing him looking at her across the table, his face open and friendly, she said, "No, I didn't. Did you?"

"Not this year. I used to make them, though."

"You did? Like what?"

"Uh-oh. How did I get myself into this?"

"Maybe you have a secret urge to confess your sins. So stop stalling and tell me."

"Okay, okay, but you have to promise you won't laugh."

"I promise."

"Well, the first resolution I remember making—I was seven—no, I think I was eight." He hesitated.

"Well?"

"I'm going to tell you, but don't even smile."

"All right, all right. I won't. Now, tell me."

"Okay. I remember writing it down on a piece of paper and putting it under my pillow at night. I swore I'd stop sucking my thumb."

Laura put her hand over her mouth to suppress a laugh.

"Hey, come on. You promised."

130

"I know. I'm not laughing. Really." She tried to make her face look serious. "But how come you still sucked your thumb when you were seven—or eight?"

"How do I know. I only did it when I watched TV and before I fell asleep at night. But I used to have this big hard blister on my thumb, and it was embarrassing."

"Well, did you stop then?"

"No, but the next year I did. I think the dentist scared me into stopping."

"Well, that wasn't so terrible. I expected something much worse. Now tell me what other resolutions you made—when you were older."

This time he wasn't smiling. "Okay, I'll tell you the last time I made a New Year's resolution. It was last year, after my father had his heart attack, and I knew how much he wanted me to become a doctor. I made a resolution that I would work really hard at school and get good grades—even if it meant that I had to become a grind to do it."

"So what happened to that resolution?"

"I just couldn't do it. It seemed so stupid to spend all that time memorizing a lot of boring stuff, and trying to do better than all my friends, and never having time to read the books *I* wanted to read—or do things that were important to *me*. So I work at the things that I really care about, but the rest—well, I do just enough to get by. And I don't make any more New Year's resolutions." He sounded angry. "My father isn't too happy about it, but I can't help it."

The waitress returned and set down plates of open-faced sandwiches. They started eating.

"I wish I could relax more about grades," Laura said. "I don't know why I have to be so good in school."

"I don't, either," Paul said. "But what about you? What kind of resolutions did you used to make?"

She hesitated. She didn't want to tell him that last year, when she started high school and knew that all her grades would be on her college records, she had made a resolution to get A's in all her classes.

"Oh, I don't really remember."

"Hey, that's not fair! I just told you all this embarrassing stuff about me. What about some of your sins? You must have had one or two in the past."

Laura remembered that awful day in her junior high French class, and her face got hot.

"Uh-oh. I think you're holding out on me. So come on—confess!"

"Well—" She stopped.

"What? I won't laugh. I promise."

"It's not that kind of thing. I mean—it wasn't funny."

"What was it, then?"

"Okay. But now you'll know much more about me than I want you to know." She took a deep breath. "I was in seventh grade and we were having a test in my French class and I didn't know the answers to some of the questions. I think it had to do with irregular verbs. Anyway, I was sitting next to Jimmy Goodman, who was a whiz in French. And when I thought the teacher couldn't see me, I copied from Jimmy's paper."

"So what happened?"

"Well, my teacher saw me. She didn't say anything in front of the class, but when I handed in my test, she asked me to stay a few minutes extra, and when everyone left, she told me she'd seen me copying from Jimmy and she was giving me an F on the test."

"Wow! What did you do?"

"I started to cry. And then I ran out of the room."

"Did she tell your parents?"

"She never had the chance. When I came home and my mother saw how upset I was, she asked me what was wrong. I burst into tears and told her. But I made her promise not to tell my father or Charlie."

Paul chewed intently on his food.

"So now you know," Laura said.

He shrugged and grinned. "Know what? That you're not perfect?"

"Far from it. And if I were making a New Year's resolution this year, I know what it would be."

"What?"

"I'd promise to be nicer to my mother."

"I didn't know you weren't nice to her."

"Well, sometimes I'm not. Especially lately." She took a bite of the last of her sandwich. "Hey," she said. "How'd we get to talking about all this stuff? We're supposed to be having fun."

"Right," Paul said. "Let's talk about something really important. What are we having for dessert?"

At The Famous Chocolate Cookie they each bought a huge brownie, and then they browsed around in the kite shop and the poster store. At Crabtree & Evelyn's, Laura sampled the perfumes. She liked the gardenia cologne the best, and sprayed a little on her neck.

"How do I smell?" she asked Paul.

He leaned close. "Not bad," he said.

"Not bad? You're supposed to say fantastic! Sensational!" She picked up the bottle again. "Now you'll smell good, too," she said, and sprayed his hair.

"Hey!" he yelled, laughing. "I'll get you for that!"

"You will, huh? How?"

"You'll see."

She followed him to Chez Chocolat. Through the glass, she watched him buy a small bag of chocolates. Outside again, he opened the bag and took out a plump dark chocolate candy. With a deliberately slow gesture, he popped the candy into his mouth.

"Mmm. Delicious," he said, and slowly walked toward the modern furniture store on the other side of the market.

As they walked along together, he took another candy out of the bag and bit into it. "I just love chocolate-covered cherries." Some of the syrup ran onto his chin. "They're my favorite." He wiped his chin with his fingers and licked them.

"Listen," Laura said. "I think it's only right that I should tell you that two people died recently after eating chocolates from that shop. The Board of Health is investigating."

"Yeah?" he said.

"Yeah," she said. "Of course, it may not be true. You know how rumors spread."

"Well, in that case, maybe you'd like one." He opened the bag. There was one candy left. "Have it," he said. "If we're gonna go, we might as well go together. Right?"

"Right." She reached into the bag. "Chocolate-covered cherries are my favorite, too."

She bit into the candy carefully, but the syrup started to spill out, so she pushed the whole thing into her mouth.

They stopped at the furniture store to look in the window at a bed with a headboard made of pale slender spindles.

"Isn't that a neat-looking bed?" Laura said.

"It's okay," Paul said. "But I wish I could lie down on it. These new boots are killing me."

"Hey, I know just the place for us," she said. "My mother took me to a pretty chapel here. Some famous artist—Louise Nevelson, I think—designed it. We could go there and sit for a while."

They moved quietly down the center aisle, taking seats together in the middle of the small room. There were only two other people in the chapel, two men, each sitting in a different pew, their heads bowed. Paul was looking at the sculptures on the walls. Then the doors opened and a young woman walked down the aisle and took a seat in the pew across the aisle from Laura.

Her blond hair was tied loosely into a bun at the nape of her neck. She stared straight ahead at the altar, and, after a few moments, wiped her eyes with a handkerchief.

Maybe she had lost a boyfriend. Or something worse. Maybe someone she really loved had died.

Laura's throat swelled up, and suddenly she had an image of what life would be like without her mother.

Laura saw herself coming home from school, cleaning up the breakfast things, and making supper for Charlie and her father. She imagined their gloomy meals—her father more silent than ever. She would try to cheer him up, but she wouldn't know what to say.

Would he get married again? If he did, she and Charlie would have a stepmother. But Laura would probably be grown up then. Maybe married, with children of her own.

"I know you're going to have lovely children," her mother had said. She had decided to lose her breast so she could live a long time. But Laura knew there were no guarantees. Some women still died.

Without her mother, Laura wouldn't have anyone to talk to when she was really upset. Her father loved her, but it was her mother she turned to when she needed comfort. And before her mastectomy, it was her mother who kept things lively at home—who helped them have fun. Her mother enjoyed life—and she was still so young.

Laura's eyes filled with tears.

She turned to Paul. He seemed to be lost in his own thoughts. But then he looked at her and took her hand.

chapter twenty-one

They were walking toward his house, and all the time he was talking, Paul was looking down at the snow-packed street.

"Oh no," Laura said. "*Arizona*? That's so far away."

"I know," Paul said.

He had come to her house after school and asked her to go for a walk. As soon as she saw his face, she knew something was wrong.

The doctors in Boston had urged his parents to move to a warmer climate. The cold weather of the Northeast was too hard on Isidor. They were thinking of Florida, but then Miriam's brother and his wife invited all of them to come and live with them in Arizona until they found their own place.

"Do they have room for you?" Laura asked.

"Yeah, they do. Their kids are grown and have moved out."

"But what'll your parents do out there?"

"It looks like there might be a job for Mom, and as soon as my father feels a bit stronger, Mom's brother has a friend who's looking for a partner to help run his drugstore."

He looked down again and gave an angry kick to a clump of snow.

"You can be sure they didn't consult me," Paul continued. "They knew about this two weeks ago but decided not to tell me till they were sure they could sell or rent the house. And then they found someone yesterday. We're leaving on Friday."

"That's the day after tomorrow."

"I know. But these people are going to rent the house for six months. And they need it right away so their kids can start school next week. My folks didn't want to turn them down."

"And you're going to do all that packing in two days?"

"We're just taking our clothes until the summer. Then they're going to try to sell the house." He turned toward her. "I'll come back to help—and—I'll see you then."

"But that's such a long time from now."

"I know."

"Oh, Paul. It's terrible. Poor you. Poor me. Poor Isidor."

"Yeah. Poor everybody. Mom thought maybe I could stay with John's family. She said she feels bad about my having to change schools again so soon—"

"Hey, that's a great idea! Do you think it would be okay with John—and his family?"

"I can't do that, Laura. Mom's going to need me. And my father needs me. If I stayed here, I'd be thinking about him all the time—worrying all the time. I'd be miserable."

"You're right," she said. "If it were my father, I'd want to be with him, too."

138

They had reached Paul's driveway. "Are you sure I should come in?" she asked. "Your parents must have a million things to do."

"They asked me to bring you back. They want to say good-bye. They like you, too, you know."

"Paul? Laura?" Miriam called when they entered the house. "We're in the kitchen."

The kitchen smelled of cinnamon and freshly baked pastry. Isidor sat at the table wearing a navy woolen bathrobe over his slacks and sweater. Miriam was bent over taking a round coffee cake out of the oven.

"That smells great," Paul said.

"I'm trying to empty the freezer." Miriam put the cake on top of the stove. "You're just in time for Sara Lee's All Butter Pecan Coffee Cake."

"After that," Isidor said, "you can have Stouffer's Veal with Lemon or Chicken à la Lean Cuisine. For breakfast we'll have our choice of Celentano's Pizza or Lasagna. Come and sit down and I'll put up some water for tea."

He started to get up, but Miriam quickly put a hand on his shoulder. "No, dear, you stay put. I'll do it."

Laura and Paul stepped over an open carton filled with cookbooks and took seats at the table.

"So—" Isidor said to Laura. "You've heard our news."

"Yes. I'm really sorry."

"Then that makes four of us," he said. "Cactus. Sand. Indian reservations. And 110 degrees in the shade. As Paul would say—yecch!"

"That's only in the summer." Miriam brought the cake to the table. "And we'll have air conditioners."

"I hate air-conditioning. I like snow and pine trees and the cold wind on my cheeks. I like winter."

"But, sweetheart," Miriam said as she cut each of them a piece of cake. "Winter doesn't like you. And, besides, we're not moving to the desert. Scottsdale is beautiful."

"I'm sure it is," Isidor said. "Did you by any chance know that we'll be arriving just in time for National Livestock Day? Isn't that exciting!"

"Come on, Izz," Miriam said. "Just think of three hundred sunny days a year. Think of oranges and grapefruits growing in your backyard. And animals we never get to see—elk and coyotes and deer and antelopes."

"'Home, home on the range,'" Isidor sang.

"And I hear they're famous for their golf courses," Miriam continued, ignoring him. "Maybe you'll take up golf when you're stronger."

"Mom," Paul said, "you're beginning to sound like the Chamber of Commerce. Maybe they'll give you a job."

"Golf?" Isidor said. "Who cares about golf? Did Mozart play golf? Did Beethoven? Bach? Brahms? Of course not. They all lived in the cold, invigorating climates of the north. I'm sure my brain is going to melt and run out of my ears and down my neck and into my belly button."

"Then Arizona will have its first meltdown," Miriam said. "You'll be famous." The kettle began to boil. "Paul, would you fix the tea?"

Miriam sat down between Laura and Isidor. "Izz, it's going to be all right," she said softly, putting her arm around him. "You'll see, honey. Really."

Isidor patted her hand. Laura looked away.

She had wanted to tell them that her chorus was going to sing part of Handel's *Messiah* in the spring, and that she had been planning to invite them to the concert. She wanted to tell them how much she was going to miss them, but she was afraid she couldn't say that without starting to cry.

"Laura." Miriam gently put her hand on top of Laura's. "Maybe you'll come and visit us. By the summer we'll have our own place, and I'm sure we'll have room for you."

"Thank you," she said. "Maybe I will."

But first she had to get through the winter. And the spring. Under the table, she counted the months on her hand, pressing each finger against her thigh. January, February, March, April, May, June. Six months.

And the money. It would probably be a few hundred dollars—round trip. Besides, so much could happen before the summer. Paul might meet another girl. Laura's throat tightened and she knew she couldn't hold back her tears much longer. She stood up.

"I have to go," she said. "And I know you have a lot to do." She reached out to shake Miriam's hand. "I'm going to miss all of you."

Miriam got up, and opening her arms wide, she drew Laura into a deep embrace.

"We'll miss you, too," she said. "All of us."

Isidor got up from his chair.

He took Laura's face in his hands and looked sadly into her eyes. "I wish I could think of something witty or clever to say, but for once, I'm at a loss for words." He kissed her on one cheek and then the other. "Be well. Stay well. You're a dear, sweet girl."

"You be well, too," Laura said, her voice barely audible.

Paul walked with her to the front door.

"When are you leaving on Friday?" she asked.

"In the morning. But we can see each other before then. What about tonight?"

"Tonight? I don't know. I've got a big test tomorrow. I've really got to study."

She saw the hurt look on his face. She didn't want to spoil their last two days together, but she didn't want to risk doing badly on her exam, either. Not now, when he was leaving her, and her only comfort would be her good grades.

"Do you have to study tomorrow night, too?" His voice was low with anger.

"No. I can see you then."

She was making a mistake. She should see him tonight and forget the test. Afterward she'd stay up all night studying.

"I'll call you tomorrow afternoon," Paul said. "We'll make plans then." He turned away from her and started down the hall.

Laura hesitated, opened the front door, and stepped out into the cold winter air.

Thursday night, Laura waited until the end of dinner to tell her family that Paul was coming over. She didn't want to have to sit through all their questions while she tried to keep from crying.

She told them what Isidor's doctors had said and about their move to Arizona the next day. When she was finished they all looked at her in silence.

Her mother put her hand on hers.

"Oh, sweetie," her mother said. "That's awful. I'm so sorry."

Laura pulled her hand away, pushed her chair back, and stood up.

"I'll be in my room. Tell Paul to come up."

*   *   *

142

She watched the driveway from her window. It had begun to snow. Tiny flakes floated into the yellow arc of the spotlight over the garage. The weather forecast was for snow all night and into the morning.

Maybe Paul's plane to Arizona would be canceled. Maybe it would be a snow day at school. Then she and Paul would have another day together.

She leaned closer to the window. There he was. His rainbow-colored scarf was wrapped around his neck, the yellow ends flapping behind him. Snowflakes glistened on his hair. He looked up at her window and waved. She waved back.

From her doorway she listened to Paul talking with her mother and father downstairs. Then she heard him on the stairs.

"Hi," she said as he came into her room carrying a small package wrapped in silver paper.

"Hi," he said, and handed her the package.

"What's this?" she asked, closing the door. "And how come?"

"It's an advance birthday present. I won't be here for it next month."

He sat down on the floor and leaned against the bed while Laura tore the wrapping paper off the package. "They're chocolate-covered cherries," he said. "From Chez Chocolat."

"Oh, hey, what a perfect present. Thank you." She kissed him on the cheek. "Don't tell me you went back to New York for these."

"No. Of course I would have—" He was grinning at her now. "But there's a Chez Chocolat store in White Plains."

"How'd you find that out?"

"I called the one in New York and asked them."

"That was really smart. Hey, you're terrific."

She opened the box and they each took a candy. Tasting the sweet chewy inside, she remembered Paul teasing her with his bag of chocolates. They'd had such a good time that day.

"I can't believe you're really leaving tomorrow," she said.

"I can't, either. It seems like we were just getting to know each other."

"I know. I had such plans for us."

"You did? Like what?"

"I'd hoped that at some point we'd have the house all to ourselves." She looked at her closed door. Paul followed her glance. "On New Year's Eve we had a chance to be alone, but you fell asleep."

"I didn't mean to," he said.

"Maybe not. But you didn't seem to mind too much."

"How do you know that? Anyway, what about last night? We could have been together last night. But you had to study."

"Yes. I had to study. What's wrong with that?"

"Plenty is wrong with that. You're so hung up on studying and stupid grades—that—"

"That what?"

"That it's more important than being with me when I'll be leaving in two days. Now it's one day." He was looking at her with the saddest eyes.

"Look, my grades will be here when you're gone, okay? They're not going to just disappear."

"But I am." Paul nodded.

Laura went over to her stereo and put on one of the CDs they had danced to on New Year's Eve.

Sitting down next to him, she took his hand. "I'm sorry, Paul. Really. I made a mistake. I should have spent last night with you. Don't be mad. I'm here with you now."

"I know," he said.

I love you, she wanted to say, but she couldn't.

"How are your folks doing?" she asked. "It must be so hard for them."

"It is. But they knew it was coming. That's why they didn't want me to bury Folly in that pet cemetery. I think they must have known then that we'd have to move."

"Are you sorry they didn't tell you before?"

"No. Not really. If I had known, well, I probably wouldn't have wanted to make friends—to get to really like someone—"

"Who could you mean?" she asked, smiling.

"Nobody you'd know," he said, smiling back.

Laura studied his face. She knew it so well now—the way he looked when he was angry or happy or sad. But if she didn't see him for a long time, there might come a day when she would close her eyes and try to see his face, and it wouldn't be there.

"I don't have a picture of you," Laura said.

"I'll send you one when we get there."

"You will? Do you promise?"

"I promise," he said. "Besides, I owe you a letter. Remember?"

Laura nodded. "I've been waiting for it."

"Well, now I'm going to finally write it. I'll e-mail it so you'll get it fast. Will you e-mail me back?"

"What do you think? But you owe me, so you write first."

"Okay. But what about a picture for me? Do you have one?"

"Nothing decent. But I'll get Rachel to take one and I'll send it to you."

The music ended and Paul got up. "I'd better go. I've still

got stuff to pack." He held out his hands to help her up. She took his hands and they stood facing each other.

He put his arms around her. "I'll miss you," he said.

"I'll miss you, too."

They kissed a long, tender kiss, and his hand moved to her breast.

"Oh, Laura," he whispered. "You feel so good."

"Yes," she murmured. "Yes."

He stroked her hair and then, much too soon, he moved away. "I've got to go," he said.

She wanted to ask him to stay—just a little longer.

He opened the door. "I'll see you."

She heard his footsteps going down the stairs.

She closed her door and leaned against it. There was a painful lump in her throat, and all at once hot tears flooded her eyes.

chapter twenty-two

Subj: No fun in Arizona
Date: 1/16
From: Folly
To: Largo

Dear Laura,

Here I am in warm and sunny Arizona and wishing I were back in cold and snowy Westchester. This is definitely not my kind of weather—or place. And so far I haven't seen a single deer or antelope playing.

I have to admit, though, that my father seems to be better already. He sits outdoors on the patio with his portable stereo and listens to his music—sometimes conducting and sometimes snoozing. He complains a lot (you know how he loves to complain), but he does seem to have much more energy. My mother, of course, is giving us the big Arizona commercials and telling us how wonderful it's going to be here. So—what can I say?

I can't say how mad I am that they made me move and change schools twice in one year. That the kids here are just as cliquey (cliquie? clickie?) as they are at Woodlands, so it's hard to make new friends—except with the weirdos who don't have any friends.

So—how are you? And how are Rachel and John doing?

I'm not going to make this a long letter because I want you to get it as soon as you turn your computer on—so you'll know I kept my word and wrote. Now it's your turn. Write back soon and I promise I'll answer right away and tell you more about what it's like here. Okay?

I wish I could make this a funnier, cleverer letter, but I'm not feeling funny or clever. I'm sure you know why.

Love,

Paul

Subj: No fun in Westchester
Date: 1/18
From: Largo
To: Folly

Dear Paul,

I just turned my computer on and there was your letter. It sure was what I needed to cheer me up. We had a big snow-storm last night so school is closed and I've been home all day, wishing I were with you in your sunny, warm Arizona, with or without the deer or the antelope playing.

I used to love snow days. But right now it's pretty gloomy at home because my mother is back on her chemotherapy this week, and it still makes her really tired and grouchy. I know what you mean about feeling you can't complain to your parents. I try to be careful what I say to my mother, but mostly I try to stay out of her way, which I know hurts her feelings. She'd like me to talk to her about the whole awful business, but I just can't do it. I sure hope the chemo is going to keep her cancer from coming back, like it's supposed to.

Rachel and John aren't doing too well. They've invited me to go to a movie with them Saturday. I guess I should say Rachel invited me. I think John would rather be alone with her. She said they had a big argument the other night. She complained that he hardly talks to her, so she doesn't know how he feels about her. He said that he just isn't a big talker, but it should be obvious that he likes her. "Action speaks louder than words," he said. In my next letter I'll give you a full report on the latest developments.

I'm glad your father is doing better. I hope it continues, even though that means you'll be living so far away. But maybe this summer I can come out to visit, like your mother said, and you can come here and visit. And, meanwhile, we can write lots of letters.

I'm going to end this now so I can send it off to you. This letter isn't funny or clever, either, and I'm sure you know why, too.

Love,
Laura

Laura sat on one side of Rachel with John on the other side. The movie was a comedy but nothing seemed very funny. She glanced over at Rachel and saw that John had his arm around her shoulders. A little later she saw John slide his hand down to Rachel's sweater. Rachel pushed his hand away.

"Aw, come on," John whispered. "Don't be so unfriendly."

"You come on," Rachel whispered back. "Just cut it out."

John folded his arms across his chest, and the next time people were laughing, he just sat there.

At the pizza place afterward, John was quieter than ever, so Laura and Rachel did most of the talking. When their pizza came, Rachel touched it lightly. "It's hot, guys," she said, "so you'd better wait a minute or you'll burn your mouth."

"Well, aren't you the cautious one," John said, and pulled a slice of pizza from the tray and slid it onto his plate. "Don't you ever like to have any fun?"

"What's the fun in getting a blister in your mouth?" Rachel said.

"Oh, you make everything into such a big deal." John took a big bite of his slice of pizza.

If it was too hot, he didn't let on, and Laura was sure he'd rather burn his whole mouth than admit Rachel was right.

Laura separated two pieces and put one on a plate for Rachel and one for herself. John reached over and took another piece for himself.

"So, have you heard from Paul?" John asked.

"Yeah, I've had one e-mail already and I think I'll be getting another one in a day or two. Are you going to write him?"

"Me? Yeah, maybe I will. Maybe he can give me some advice on how to thaw a certain prude we both happen to know."

"Prude?" Rachel said. "Thanks a lot."

"Well, what word would you use?" John said. "What do you call someone who has all kinds of rules—who can't let herself enjoy life."

"John, do we have to have this conversation right here? I don't think Laura is very interested in this."

But Laura was interested. Rachel didn't know how lucky

she was to have a boyfriend who wanted to do more than hold hands and kiss.

"Sorry, Laura," John said. "Anyway, when you write Paul next time, say hello for me and tell him that I miss him."

Every day Laura turned on her computer to see if she had an e-mail from Paul, but each day she was disappointed. She thought of sending him an e-mail, anyway, but she decided to be patient and just wait till his letter came before writing back.

It was more than two weeks since she had written to Paul when Rachel called her.

"You're not going to believe this," Rachel said.

"What? Did John finally call and apologize?"

"You must be dreaming. He still hasn't called. And I was beginning to think that since John isn't the kind of guy to say he's sorry, maybe I'd call him and ask him how he was and well, you know, forget about all the stupid things he said."

"Good idea. So, did you?"

"No, not after what I just found out."

"What? What?"

"You know Jennifer—that really tall girl in my French class? Well, she told me that her cousin goes to Woodlands, and listen to this. Her cousin's going out with John now. He took her to a basketball game and to the movies, and he's hanging around with her all the time."

"You're kidding."

"I'm not. You know, if he had told me he thought we should break up, I wouldn't have really minded. I mean— I was thinking it wasn't going to work for us and maybe

151

we should break up. But to just do it without saying any-thing—"

"What a rat," Laura said. "You deserve better than that, Rache."

"Yeah, I think so, too. So that's my news. What about you? Did you hear from Paul yet?"

"No, not yet."

"Well, you will—soon. I know you will."

chapter twenty-three

Laura read her report card one more time. There was the row of four A's, and—still, still, still—that one B in social studies. Everything was ruined.

Now she would continue to be what she had always been. Nothing-special Laura. Smart, but not brilliant. And not gifted like her brother. Pretty, but not beautiful. Popular? Well, she did have a boyfriend, but he'd been gone three weeks and still hadn't answered her e-mail. Maybe he didn't like her that much in the first place. And it was because of him that she ended up with that one B.

The night before the social studies test, all the time she had been trying to study, her mind had been on Paul. She had been so mad at herself for not being able to forget about schoolwork for once.

She knew she hadn't done well on the test, but she didn't expect the C that Mr. Reynolds gave her, or his comment written next to the grade: "This isn't up to your usual good work, Laura. What happened?"

Well, she certainly wasn't going to tell Mr. Reynolds about her love life. And anyway, since he remembered all her "usual good work," she had thought he would be generous and give her an A minus for the course. No such luck.

Now she had to get one of her parents to sign the report card. If she asked her mother to sign it, her mother would say that they were fine grades, and she would probably mean it. But she'd see how upset Laura was over the B, and she'd be bound to make some comment about her being too hard on herself. She'd be safer with her father.

She looked for him in the living room. Only Charlie was there, practicing the piano, playing that beautiful Bach prelude she liked so much. Whatever he had gotten on his report card, it didn't seem to bother him. He was already planning to go to the Alternative School when he started high school.

She wondered what the Alternative School was really like. She knew that you didn't get grades there. Maybe she ought to talk to some of the kids she knew who went there. If she had been in the Alternative School, she was sure she would have spent the two last nights with Paul.

She found her father in the den putting a fresh coat of white paint on the inside of the door. He was wearing his old paint clothes and newspaper was spread out on the floor.

"Hi, pal," he said. "Be careful, don't touch." Then, seeing the piece of paper in her hand, he said, "If that's a bill, tear it up and tell whoever sent it to forget it. The cupboard is bare."

"It's not a bill, Dad. But is the cupboard really bare?"

"No. Not really. But this is a rough month." He waved his hand at the papers on his desk. "I just paid five hundred dollars to Dr. Brody. You kids must have more cavities than teeth."

"Sorry about that," Laura said. "You gotta sign this, but it won't cost you any money."

Putting his brush down on the edge of the paint can, he took the paper from her. "Hey, kid, I'm really proud of you." He got a pen from his desk and signed his name at the bottom of the paper. "That's really good."

"It's not so good," she said.

He handed it back to her. "Because of the B?"

"Yeah."

"You were hoping for all A's?"

"I should've been able to get them, but—"

"But what? Unfair teachers?"

"No—"

"What, then?"

She didn't answer.

Her father looked at her thoughtfully. "Listen, I hate to start a sentence with 'When I was your age' but, when I was sixteen, and my father lost his job, my grades *really* went down. If I got a B, I was lucky, but, eventually, my grades went back up. The heart mends, sweetie. Yours will, too."

"It's not the same, Dad," she said, feeling herself blush. "No one died."

"I know, but it probably feels as though someone did." He turned away from her and dipped his paintbrush into the can. "Anyway," he continued, "that's a really good report card. Have you shown it to Mom?"

"No. Not yet." She tucked the card into the rear pocket of her jeans.

"Well, be sure you do."

Her mother was in her bedroom, rearranging things in one of her dresser drawers. "Hi," she said. "Oh, you got your report card, too." She read it quickly and handed it back to Laura. "Those are really fine grades. I'm proud of you. But you don't look pleased."

"I guess they're okay," Laura said, and changed the subject. "That's what I should be doing—going over my drawers. They're a real mess."

"Mine are, too."

Laura knew that couldn't be true.

"Since I have to get rid of my old bras, I figured I might as well do a job on the whole drawer."

"Why can't you use your old bras?"

"Because I've gotten new ones that have a pocket inside to hold my prosthesis."

Laura flinched.

"I know—that's an awful-sounding word. But they make really natural-looking ones these days. Do you want to see what it looks like?"

Laura didn't answer at first. Finally, she said, "Mom, I'm sorry, but—well, I guess not now. Not yet."

Her mother took out her old bras and piled them on the top of her dresser. Laura noticed for the first time the circles under her mother's eyes.

"That's okay," her mother said. "This thing is hard on everyone. I forget sometimes that we all need time to get used to it." She gave Laura a sad smile.

"I think I'll work on my drawers, too," Laura said.

But back in her room, she didn't want to do that. She needed to do something to ease the awful feelings that welled up in her every time she disappointed her mother.

Maybe if she put on some music, that would cheer her up. But looking through her CDs, she couldn't find one that appealed to her. Then she remembered that Charlie had just bought a Flying Hamsters CD. Maybe he'd lend it to her.

Charlie had a new sign on his door: WIPE OUT MENTAL ILLNESS OR I'LL KILL YOU.

Laura smiled. Charlie always found things to laugh about.

His room was dark, and something smelled sweet and minty. "Hey, what's going on?" she asked.

"Close the door," Charlie said. "Sit down, here—on my bed—and watch."

He stood silhouetted against the dim light coming through his drawn curtains.

Laura heard a crunching sound. The sweet, minty odor became stronger, and a glow of tiny white sparks shot from Charlie's mouth. There were more crunching sounds and more sparks.

He switched on his desk light and holding a mirror in his hand, he stood facing her.

"Pretty neat, huh?" He grinned at her.

"How'd you do that?"

"I chewed wintergreen Life Savers. They give off sparks. It's called—" He picked up a newspaper clipping on his desk. "It's called *triboluminescence*. I saw this article about it the other day. Wouldn't it be cool to use these at one of my piano concerts? Talk about special effects. I can see it now. 'Charlie the Pianist. His performances are electrifying.'"

"I can't wait to see it live," Laura said.

"Want to try it?" Charlie asked, holding out a Life Saver.

"Thanks, but I'm not exactly in the mood. What I'm really in the mood for is your new Flying Hamsters CD. Can I borrow it?"

"I don't know. Perhaps for a small fee . . ."

"Oh, Charlie." Laura sighed. "Just forget it." She turned to leave.

"Hey, wait," he called. "I was only joking."

"I know. I'm sorry. I'm just having a bad day."

"Hmm, in that case, you need more than the Flying Hamsters." He picked up his guitar. "You need . . . me, Charles Gould, brother extraordinaire, to cheer you up."

"Don't try for the impossible," Laura said.

"Give me a chance, big sister," he said. "How about we send out for pizza?"

"Does pizza help with boyfriend pains?" Laura asked.

"Well, I hear it can replace heartache with heartburn. Give it a try."

Laura giggled. Charlie giggled, too.

Charlie strummed out a chord. "Friends, Romans, and Laura. Lend me your ears." He played out the chords for "On Top of Old Smokey" and began to sing.

"On top of your pizza,
All covered with cheese,
We'll put on some hot dogs,
And French fries to please.

"We'll add on some egg rolls,
And some whipped cream, too.
And if you don't like it,
I'll eat it for you."

"Stop!" Laura said, laughing. "You're making me sick."

"Okay, okay. We'll leave off the cheese."

They both giggled again.

"So," Charlie said, "anyone for pizza?"

Laura shook her head. "I'll pass, but the heartache does feel a little bit better, thanks to you."

"Only a little bit better? I guess the Flying Hamsters will have to do the rest."

He handed her the CD, and she gave him a hug. "Thanks, Charlie. If I'm in need of pizza and a song later, I know who to come to."

"You bring the money for the pizza, and I'll provide the entertainment."

"Deal."

With her door closed and the CD on her stereo, Laura stretched out on her bed. It was fun kidding around with Charlie. She hadn't laughed like that for ages. So even though he was such a whiz on the piano, and she would probably always be jealous of him for that, he was Charlie, her brother, funny and sweet and kind.

The Flying Hamsters was one of her favorite groups. She tried to think about the words to the song they were singing, but somehow thoughts about Paul kept intruding. She still couldn't understand why she hadn't heard from him. He'd written "Write back soon and I'll answer right away." She knew his letter by heart. And she had answered right away.

Maybe his father's heart was bad again and he was too upset to write about it. Maybe that was it. She'd write and ask him.

She went to her desk and turned on her computer.

Subj: Waiting for a letter
Date: 2/4
From: Largo
To: Folly

Dear Paul,

I've been waiting for a letter from you for more than two weeks. What happened? I hope it's not because your father is having a hard time again. I was so glad when you wrote that he's better—and I sure hope that's still true.

Anyway, please write soon and tell me what's going on with you. You know—how your new school is and what the kids are like. And, of course, how your father is doing.

Nothing much is new here—except the latest with Rachel and John. They've broken up. Or rather John, without saying anything to Rachel, stopped calling her or seeing her and is now going with a girl from his school. What do you think of that?

She stopped writing. Paul could have met a girl he liked out there. A girl who was more his type. Who wasn't so far away.

Of course. That was it.

She was so stupid not to have figured it out before.

She pushed the delete key until the letter disappeared.

chapter twenty-four

Ten minutes. Ten stupid minutes. If Laura had come home from Rachel's house just ten minutes sooner, she would have been there for Paul's call.

"Tell me what he said. His exact words."

"Again?" Charlie said as he put his dishes in the dishwasher. "Not even my piano teacher asks me to repeat things so many times. He asked if you were home, and when I said you weren't, he just said 'Well, tell her I called,' and hung up."

"Come on. Think. He must have said more than that."

"I'm telling you—that's all he said, but he sounded kind of weird."

"How do you mean 'weird'?"

"Weird. Strange. Bizarre. Maybe he was mad you weren't home. Or maybe he was being held hostage by Arizona aliens. How should I know?"

"I wish you had asked him for his phone number."

"I told you ten times—he didn't give me a chance."

If only her mother had been home. She would have gotten him to say more—or at least have found out where she could call him back. Well, maybe she could get his phone number from information. The Rosens had been there a month now, so maybe they had their own phone. She went upstairs to use the phone in her parents' room.

It was complicated, but she finally got Scottsdale information. There was no listing for Isidor or Miriam Rosen. And she didn't know the name of Miriam's brother.

Several times she had thought of going over to Paul's house and asking for the Rosens' phone number, but she could never bring herself to do it. Well, maybe Paul would call again. And if he didn't, he'd certainly send her another e-mail.

But he didn't call back, and no e-mail came.

One night, a week later, she stood outside her house and looked up at a clear sky filled with stars. She was coming home from the library, and somehow she was reluctant to go inside. The cold, wintry air made the stars sparkle with a special brilliance—like they had the night she and her mother had made wishes on the two shooting stars.

Those wishes hadn't come true. Instead, the stars brought bad news to her mother, to Isidor, to all of them. Wishing on stars was a silly thing to do. Nothing had helped her mother or Isidor, and nothing was going to help her hear from Paul.

"Laura, is that you?" her father called when she finally went into the house.

Her father was sitting on the couch in the living room, a book on his lap. Laura dumped her library books on a chair and took off her jacket.

He looked up at her. "What's the matter, honey?"

"Nothing," she said. "What makes you think something's the matter?"

"I don't know. You don't look like your usual cheerful self. But then, I guess you haven't looked like that for a while."

"I'm okay," she said. "Just a little cold. It's a real wintry night out there."

He patted the cushion on the couch next to him. "Come sit here," he said, "and I'll warm you up. I hope you haven't gotten too grown-up for a little cuddling from your old man."

He put his arm around her and gently rubbed her shoulder.

"Where's Mom?" she asked.

"She went to pick up Charlie at Michael's," he said.

Laura sighed. She'd tell her father and get it over with.

"Well, you're right, Dad. I guess I don't feel very cheerful these days. Paul hasn't written me for over two weeks."

"Really? But didn't he call you a while ago?"

"He did, but I wasn't home, and he didn't call back. I wrote him last and he never wrote back, either."

"Oh, sweetie, don't make rules about who writes to who—oops—whom. He's in a new school and a new place and maybe feeling overwhelmed. There may be a perfectly good reason why he hasn't written."

"That's just it. I think there is a reason. I think he must have met someone—someone he likes, and he's afraid to tell me. Maybe he was going to tell me when he called, but then he lost his nerve."

"That doesn't sound like him. He's kind of shy, and maybe you don't know it, but I know something about people like that." He smiled at her. "Don't give up on Paul."

"But I think he's given up on me."

"But maybe he hasn't. Swallow your pride and write again."

She stood up. "You're right. I'll give it another try."

Date: 2/12
Subj: Still waiting, but hopeful
From: Largo
To: Folly

Dear Paul,

I'm still waiting for a letter from you. I know you called, and I was so disappointed that I wasn't here. I thought you'd call again, or at least write, but you haven't.

If you're glad to hear from me, you can thank my father. In one of the longest conversations I think I ever had with him, he told me I shouldn't give up on you. He has always been a shy guy, and maybe you're like him. Anyway, he says you probably have a perfectly good reason for taking so long to write.

Do you?

She stopped writing and pictured Paul with another girl. She was probably very pretty—much prettier than she was. Did he kiss her? Did he do things with this girl that he never did with her? Maybe she was able to help him get over his shyness. Did he tell her about his girlfriend back in the East? She was nice, he'd tell her, but not like you.

Swallow your pride, her father had said. Well, that was easy for him to say. She couldn't swallow it, and she wasn't going to make a fool of herself by begging Paul to write her.

Once again she deleted everything she had written.

"Hey, why'd you pick such an expensive place?" Laura asked as they read their menus.

"This is your birthday present," Rachel said. "You're not supposed to look at the prices."

"But I feel guilty having you spend so much money."

"Listen, this is a treat for me, too. But you can pay me back when you get your license. I expect rides all over the place. When are you getting your learner's permit?"

"Monday. Mom's picking me up at school and driving me to the motor vehicle place."

"Is your mother going to teach you to drive?"

"No. She says she'll be too nervous. My father's going to do it. Oh, I hope I pass the test the first time!"

"You will. You will. Then—freedom! You're so lucky. I have to wait till June."

"I don't feel so lucky," Laura said.

"What's the matter?" Rachel asked. "Still upset over Paul?"

"I guess so."

"I still can't believe he hasn't written."

"Well, believe it."

"Hey, let's try not to think about it today. Are you doing something special tonight with your family?"

"My mother's making a special birthday dinner for me. She wanted to throw me a party—I guess sixteen is still supposed to be a big deal—but I'm sure not in the mood for a party. I'm not in the mood for anything."

"Listen," Rachel said. "I just got a terrific idea."

"Great. I'd be happy with a mediocre idea."

"We're going to Jamaica for the school break. Maybe you could come with us. That's what you need—to get away."

Jamaica. Hot sun. Lying on the beach—getting a tan. That would be so nice. But getting there would cost so much.

"Thanks, Rachel, that's so nice of you to ask me, but I couldn't."

"Why not? Because of the money? All you'd need is the airfare. You could share my room, and I'm sure my parents would treat you to the meals. Think about it."

"It's a great idea, but I know I couldn't. Money is kind of tight in our house right now. My father was expecting a bonus, but his firm isn't doing so well, so now, no bonus."

When Paul left, Laura had been thinking of telling her parents that all she wanted for her birthday was money to fly out to Arizona during one of her school vacations. Now she was glad she hadn't said anything to them about it.

"Thanks for asking me," she said, touching Rachel on her hand. "You're a good friend."

Laura's mother made meatballs and spaghetti, something Laura really liked, and she had even made a chocolate birthday cake from scratch. They all sang "Happy Birthday" to her as her mother brought the cake with the lighted candles into the dining room. They usually ate there only when they had company. Her mother was trying really hard to make it a special birthday. When it was time for her to make a wish, as she blew out the candles, Laura had an uncomfortable feeling that everyone there knew what she was wishing.

Her mother's present to her was just what Laura wanted—money. Inside her birthday card were ten crisp ten dollar bills.

"I know you like to go with your friends to pick out clothes," she said.

Charlie gave her two Flying Hamsters CDs. And her father had handed her an envelope with a poem inside. She went around the table thanking them and kissing each of them on the cheek.

Later that night, sitting at her desk, she read her father's poem again.

LAURA THE LION

Laura the Lion lies in her lair
Brushing back her lion's hair.

She smiles and offers up her chin
For tickling and a lion's grin
But soon she'll leave the lion's den—
Will she ever, oh, ever, return again?

The lion's grown so tall and proud,
No more tickling chins allowed.

Underneath the poem he had written: Happy Birthday to My Sweet, Sweet Laura.

When she was a little girl her father used to make up funny stories and tell them to her while he was shaving. She would sit on the edge of the bathtub and listen while she watched his razor slice off globs of shaving cream. Her favorite story was the one about Laura the Lion. And now he had written her favorite story into a poem about her.

Paul hadn't written, and the thought that despite her birthday wish, maybe he wasn't ever going to write was more than she could bear. But her birthday—starting with Rachel—had been a nice day. She was lucky. She had a good friend and a family that loved her.

If only she could be satisfied with that.

chapter twenty-five

Laura drove down the street and pulled into her driveway. It was a cold Friday afternoon in the end of February, and just a few days ago she had passed her driving test on the first try. Now, with her father in Chicago on business for a few days, she had the wonderful luxury of driving his car to school.

Getting her license was the first thing that had lifted her spirits in ages. She had just made plans to go driving with Rachel on Saturday. They were going to the mall for lunch and shopping.

Inside, her mother was at the kitchen table reading a magazine. A cup of tea and the day's mail were in front of her. Although the pile of letters looked like the usual assortment of bills and requests for contributions, Laura felt a flicker of hope. Maybe Paul had decided to write a regular letter to her and it was right there in the pile.

Well, she wouldn't look through it with her mother watching her, feeling sorry for her.

"There's a card for you from Dad," her mother said, handing her a postcard.

Laura set her books down on the table and took the card. On one side was a picture of Lake Michigan. On the other side her father had written:

The winds from the lake in this windy city
Have blown out my brains and I can't be witty.
I miss my driving companion.
Love, Dad

"Did he send you and Charlie a card?" Laura asked.

"Yes. I guess he misses us."

Her mother took her cup and saucer to the sink. "It's going to be just you and me for dinner tonight. Charlie's sleeping over at Michael's. I got some filet of sole and artichokes. How does that sound?"

"Great." Those were things that only the two of them liked.

Dinner with just her mother might be strange, though. They hadn't been alone together for a long time.

While her father was teaching her to drive, Laura had spent a lot of time with him. He was easy to be with. He didn't ask questions, and he didn't expect her to confide in him. It was different with her mother. Laura felt that her mother always wished Laura would tell her more. But there was nothing Laura could tell her. Nothing. That's what her life was these days. One big nothing.

Dinner went better than she expected, and afterward her mother sat at the table, looking at the TV schedule in the newspaper. "Hey, you know what's on TV tonight?" she asked.

"What?"

169

"*Brief Encounter.* My all-time favorite movie."

"Is that the one you've seen twenty times?"

"Only ten, I think. It's a wonderful love story about a married woman who meets a man—a doctor, who's also married—and they fall in love in England, right after World War II. Want to watch it with me?"

It didn't sound like Laura's kind of movie. On the other hand, it would be an easy way of spending some time with her mother. It might help make up for all the times she had avoided being alone with her.

"Okay," Laura said.

Her mother was stretched out on the couch, her head propped up on two cushions. Laura sat across from her, her legs hanging over the arm of the club chair.

"What's that music in the background?" Laura asked.

"Rachmaninoff. It's beautiful, isn't it?"

At first Laura found it hard to be interested in the movie. But after a while the characters became people she cared about, people she felt she knew.

"*Do you think we shall ever see each other again?*"

"*I don't know. Not for years, anyway.*"

"*The children will all be grown-up . . . I wonder if they'll meet and know each other.*"

"*Couldn't I write to you . . . just once in a while?*"

Tears filled Laura's eyes, blurring her vision. Reaching for the box of tissues on the end table, she saw that her mother was crying, too.

The movie ended and Laura turned off the TV. Suddenly, she was crying again. Tears flowed down her cheeks and her nose began to run.

Her mother handed her the box of tissues. "Come sit with me, honey." She patted the space on the couch.

Laura sat next to her and wiped her tears and blew her nose.

And then sobs filled her throat and as they spilled out, she buried her face on her mother's shoulder.

"It's so awful," she cried. "I miss him so much."

"I know," her mother said softly as she stroked Laura's hair.

"How could he forget about me?"

"Oh, honey, I'm sure he didn't forget you."

"He must have. And you know, it's not just Paul I miss. I miss his whole family. They were so nice. I wanted you to meet them. You'd really like Miriam, Paul's mother. And Isidor, Paul's father. He knows all about music, and he's got the wildest sense of humor. You'd love him."

"Well, you said they were coming back in June to get all their things. Maybe I can meet them then."

"Not if Paul's lost interest in me."

"I'm sure he hasn't. There must be a reason he hasn't written. But I'm sure you'll hear from him soon. Hand me a tissue, sweetie."

"Why were you crying, Mom?" Laura asked.

"I don't know. Maybe because I feel that someday I might lose someone I love—that nothing lasts forever."

Laura nodded. "Mom, are you all right now? I mean—your cancer. Are you cured?"

"Well, the doctor says my chances of being okay are very good, and the chemotherapy is making them even better. And I haven't lost any hair. I guess my luck is changing."

"Take care of yourself, Mom."

"I'm doing the best I can, sweetie. I think I'm going to be fine now. Really."

"Mom—"

"What?"

"I'm sorry I've been such a crab these past few weeks."

Her mother smiled at her. "Months," she said.

"Months? Really?"

"Yes. But I know you've been having a hard time, too. I wish I could do something to help."

"I wish you could, too."

chapter twenty-six

Rachel answered on the first ring.

"Where were you all day?" Laura asked, kicking off her shoes and stretching out on her parents' bed.

"I'm sick, darn it."

"What've you got?"

"A sore throat and fever. My mother took a culture. She thinks I have strep."

"Oh no. How do you feel?"

"Not too bad, unless I try to swallow. Then I feel suicidal."

"Please. Suicide is out—at least until June. I don't think I could get through the rest of school without you."

"Thanks. I guess you had a great day."

"The greatest. Baker announced a test on the last three chapters, and Mrs. Forrest assigned a ten-page paper for Monday."

"Boy, I'm glad I wasn't there."

"All they do is pile it on. So—I've been thinking—"

"You gotta stop doing that, Laura."

"Very funny. Be serious a minute. I've been thinking about applying to the Alternative School for next year."

"You have? I thought you said you weren't interested."

"Well, I thought I wasn't. But I think I had the wrong idea about the school. I mean, I used to think it was just for kids who couldn't make it in the regular high school—you know, kids with learning problems—but it isn't."

"How do you know?"

"I was talking to Beth yesterday, and her brother is a senior there, and he just got into Yale—and another kid is going to Brown. Her brother loves it. And today, Charlie came home with some stuff about it."

"What kind of stuff?"

"Oh you know—stuff about their philosophy—and how you make these contracts for each subject with your teachers. The thing I like best is that the teachers write you evaluations instead of giving you grades. I know I spend much too much time worrying about those stupid letters on a piece of paper. I want to enjoy school."

"Hey, who are you, and what have you done with Laura?"

"I'm serious, Rache. I even spent some of the time just before Paul left studying for a test instead of being with him. What a stupid jerk I was!"

"Well, if you're considering it," Rachel said, "I guess I should, too. I sure don't want to be at the regular school without you. What do your parents say?"

"I haven't talked to them about it yet, but I'm going to. Charlie's planning to go to the Alternative School, so I think they'll like the idea of my going there, too. But you talk to your parents, okay?"

"Okay."

"Oh, hey, I almost forgot. Guess who I saw at the basketball game."

"Who?" Rachel asked.

"John. We played Woodlands today."

"Did you talk to him?"

"No. He was on the other side of the court. Anyway, what would I have said?"

"Maybe he's heard from Paul. Maybe he could explain why Paul hasn't written."

"Listen, if Paul wrote him and not me, what could there be to explain?"

"You're right. Forget I said anything."

"Don't worry. That's my specialty these days—forgetting." Then Laura said, "Do you miss John?"

"Sometimes."

"Only sometimes? You're lucky."

Before dinner that night, while Laura set the table and her mother made a salad, Laura told her mother about her idea of going to the Alternative School in the fall. Just as she had expected, her mother thought it was a good idea.

"Tom and Rita's daughter, Sarah, has been there for a couple of years, and I hear she really likes it. And Charlie wants to go there when he starts high school."

"I know," Laura said.

"Well, I guess we need to find out how you apply. But listen, I wanted to ask you something. You know this support group that I go to for women who've had breast cancer—"

"Yeah, what's it called?"

"Women Helping Women. They're having a meeting on Friday at the Y. It's for mothers and daughters. Would you come along with me?"

Laura hesitated. She wished she could say no, but, of course, she couldn't.

"I'd be glad to go," she said, feeling anything but glad. It would probably just end up making her feel more guilty. Then again, maybe there'd be other daughters who were like her.

Laura counted fifteen people sitting in chairs arranged in a circle. Coffee and tea and sodas and a plate of cookies were on a table nearby. Some of the women looked quite old to Laura, and their daughters seemed almost as old as Laura's mother. There were two girls about Laura's age. A social worker named Doris led the group.

"Well, let's get started," Doris said. "I think we all know this is a difficult time, not only for the women who have breast cancer but for everyone in their family—and especially for their daughters. So, let's talk about the problems some of you may have had, and the good things that have been part of the mother-daughter relationships. I hope we can all learn from one another. Who would like to begin?"

They all shifted uncomfortably in their seats. Then one of the mothers said, "I'll start. I'm so glad to be here because I want to publicly thank my daughter, Judy, for being so supportive and helpful. My husband died five years ago, and I don't think I could have survived without Judy." She put her arm around the girl sitting next to her and kissed her. The girl, who looked about eighteen, blushed. "Thank you, Mom," she said. "I think you're pretty terrific yourself. And very brave."

Oh, great, Laura thought. Is this what the whole night was going to be like?

Another woman spoke. She was younger, and the girl sitting next to her looked to be about twelve or thirteen. "I wish I could say the same thing," the woman said. "But I can't. My husband left me a few months after my mastectomy, and I know that's been upsetting to Jennifer. But I don't really know how she feels because she's over at her friends' houses all the time and never wants to talk to me."

Jennifer folded her arms and, after a moment's hesitation, said, "You're not fair, Mom, and it's not true. You expect too much from me."

"But you're my daughter," the woman said. "I don't think you're too young to understand how devastating a mastectomy is for me."

After a short silence a middle-aged woman started to speak. "I've never been to group like this," she said. "Unfortunately, there wasn't anything like this when my mother died twenty years ago. Maybe if there had been, I wouldn't have spent twenty years feeling so sad and guilty about the way I acted when she was so sick." Her eyes filled with tears and she took out a tissue from her pocketbook and wiped her eyes.

"How old were you when your mother died?" Doris asked.

"I had just turned twenty and my mother had been sick for about three years. They hadn't caught her cancer early, so it was too late to save her. Even though I was an adult, I was angry at her for being sick, for leaving me—for dying. And for making me feel so frightened that it might happen to me. I loved my mother, but I must have hurt her so much. So— that's why I decided to come tonight. I hope to help some of you understand your feelings before it's too late."

*   *   *

For the first few minutes going home, Laura and her mother drove in silence.

"Mom," Laura finally said softly. "That woman, the one who told us about how angry she felt when her mother was so sick. I guess she was like me."

"I guess she was," her mother said.

"I'm sorry, Mom. I really am."

"I know, honey. I'm sorry, too. This whole thing is much harder on everyone than most people realize." She put her hand on Laura's.

"What would I do without you, Mom?"

"Luckily, I don't think that's going to be a problem. I expect to be around for a long, long time."

"It's so unfair," Laura said. "Why does something like that happen?"

"I don't know, sweetie. I suppose there are reasons, causes, and someday I'm sure doctors will find a way to prevent it. Meanwhile, surviving and making the most of my life seems to be the best thing to try to do."

"How much longer do you have to have the chemotherapy?"

"Another five months."

"That's a long time."

"I know. But I don't mind it so much anymore. The first day I have the injection is pretty bad, and I hate feeling crummy the two weeks I'm on the stuff. But now I think of it as a gift."

"A gift?"

"It's a gift from science—from medicine—to help me live longer. That's what's really important to me. I want to stick around for a long time and enjoy my family."

They drove the rest of the way home in comfortable silence. When they pulled into the driveway, Laura said, "Mom, I just got a great idea. I want to take you out to lunch tomorrow. My treat."

"Really? That *is* a great idea." She turned off the engine. "But you don't have to do that. It can be my treat."

"No. Not this time. This time I want to pay. I still have some of my birthday money left, so let's go to someplace really nice. You choose."

"Wow. I don't know what to say."

"Say yes, and tell me where you'd like to go."

"Well, how about Mary Lou's? I love it there with all the plants and flowers." And then suddenly she was crying.

"Mom, what's the matter?"

"I'm just so happy. Happy to have you for a daughter— and happy to be alive."

Laura slept late on Saturday morning and when she got up she felt more cheerful than she had in a long time. She had to do some homework, but she could do that after her lunch out with her mother. After she had a hot shower, she felt even better.

She took out the new yellow sweater she'd bought with her birthday money. While she was getting dressed she sang her favorite part of Handel's *Messiah*. She had been rehearsing it in school for the spring concert.

"'Hallelujah! Hallelujah! Hallelujah! Hal-le-lu-jah!'"

As she sang, she remembered how she had been planning to invite the Rosens to her concert, knowing Isidor would especially love the music.

Isidor.

How was he doing?

She went to her desk and sat on the chair and stared into space. After a few minutes she turned on the computer.

Subj: Needing to Know
Date: 3/13
From: Largo
To: Folly

Dear Paul,

I know you said you'd answer my letter right away, and when I didn't hear from you I was really hurt. And angry. I just couldn't understand it, and I finally decided that you must have found another girlfriend. And maybe that is the reason. But, today, I suddenly realized that there might be another reason.

Maybe the reason you haven't written is because your father had another heart attack.

So, Paul, please write and tell me how your father is. And how you are. And your mother. And if you need to tell me that you're not interested in me anymore, you can tell me that, too. But let me hear from you. Please. If you still do have some interest in me—and you're wondering how I am—except for missing you, I'm fine. My mother's also fine, and I know how lucky I am to have her. Paul, I hope you're lucky, too.

Love,

Laura

"Laura, I'm ready when you are," her mother called.

"I'll be right there, Mom." Turning back to her computer, she clicked on Send.

chapter twenty-seven

Five days later she saw him. On a sudden impulse she had decided to ride her bike down Paul's street, and there he was, walking a small black dog, a Scottie. Paul's back was to her, and she pedaled hard to catch up to him.

He had come back to get some things from his house. He had gotten her letter and decided to surprise her. He was on his way to her house now—to explain everything. He had missed her so much that it was just too painful to write. His parents had gotten him the Scottie to cheer him up. A Scottie from Scottsdale. Of course.

No. There was another reason. His father was better, and now that the cold weather was almost over, they had decided to move back, at least until next winter. He wanted to give her the news in person.

She pedaled faster. But coming closer she saw that his hair was a lighter brown. Well, the Arizona sun could to that. But his walk was different, too.

She slowed down. There had been lots of other times she thought she had seen him. At the movies, in the supermarket, even in school, where she knew he wouldn't be. Each time as she had gotten closer to him and he had turned around, she had looked into the face of a stranger.

Now she saw that he was taller, too. She rode slowly past him.

"Hi," the boy said.

He didn't even look like Paul.

"Hi," she called back, and heavy with disappointment, she continued pedaling.

He wasn't coming back. He wasn't going to answer her letter. She just had to face it. It was all over.

Every night she turned on her computer to check her e-mail. Well, today she wouldn't do it. She'd cure herself of that habit.

She put her bike in the garage and went into the house. Her mother was at the kitchen sink peeling some carrots.

Laura dumped her books on the table. Her mother gave her a big smile.

"There's mail for you," her mother said, and the smile got bigger.

"Mail?" A hot jolt of excitement swept through her.

"Yes. Mail. It's the thing the postman brings—in sleet or snow or black of night . . ."

She took an envelope out of the mail basket and handed it to Laura.

There was Paul's handwriting. She turned the envelope over. Paul Rosen, it said on the flap. Underneath his name was his address in Scottsdale, Arizona.

"Thanks, Mom."

Laura picked up her books and left the kitchen. With each step up the stairs, she imagined a different letter.

Dear Laura,
I haven't written because I didn't want to hurt you, but I have to tell you that I've met someone out here and . . .

Dear Laura,
I haven't written because I've been so mad at you for the way things ended with us—and I guess things really are ended . . .

Dear Laura, . . .

She quietly closed her bedroom door, set her books down on her desk, and sat down in her chair. She stared at the envelope. Finally, she slid her finger under the flap.

Dear Laura,
I got your letter two days ago, and I can't tell you how happy I was to hear from you. I was hoping you'd write, even though I know I promised to write again soon. Laura, please don't be angry with me. I just couldn't write. And what I have to tell you I just couldn't put in an e-mail.

My wonderful father is dead. He died a month ago—on February 6.

Like I told you, he seemed fine for the first week or so that we were out here, and then he got bad again. He was in the hospital for two weeks, and then it looked like he was going to be okay. But one morning while he was home, he had a massive heart attack. He died the next day in the hospital. Mom and I were sitting next to him, holding his hands, but he didn't know that.

I can't write any more about it now. It's still too hard. And it's still so unreal. I just can't believe it. At dinnertime, I still expect him to walk into the kitchen and sit down at the table with us. And when I listen to some of the music he was always playing, and I can't remember what it is, I think—oh, I'll ask Pop. He'll know.

So, now you know why I haven't written. I haven't forgotten you. I think about you all the time—wishing you were here with me. And I've wanted to write—but while he was so sick—I just couldn't. Did Charlie tell you I called? It was the day after Pop died. When you weren't home I decided to write you and tell you what happened, but then I couldn't. If you're having trouble understanding why, I wouldn't blame you, because I am, too. Maybe writing about it would make it too real. Too permanent. But I've missed you so much—and I've wanted to hear from you so badly—so I guess you still are Miss Psychic, because you sure read my mind.

I'm saving the one good piece of news for last. Are you ready? We're coming back! As soon as the school term is over, and the people move out of our house in Hartsdale, we're moving back. Mom will have her job back at Harmony House. And I'll start looking for a summer job that pays some money.

Mom sends her love. She misses you, too.

I guess you haven't found another boyfriend. Whew! But if there's someone else hanging around—and I can't believe there isn't—don't tell me. (Just shoot him.) Please write again soon. Really soon!

Love, Paul

Laura leaned back in her chair and saw Paul in a hospital room, holding his father's hand. She swallowed hard.

She'd see Paul again. But Isidor—

She saw him standing in front of his stereo, conducting

Don Giovanni. She saw Miriam with her arms around him in their kitchen, telling him it was going to be all right.

She read the letter again and tears welled up in her eyes.

Paul was wrong. She wasn't Miss Psychic at all. She should have written him right away when she didn't hear from him. She had almost failed him. And she had almost failed her mother, too.

And Isidor—she'd never see him again. The tears ran down her cheeks.

She put the letter on her bed and opened her door. "Mom," she called out.

"What is it?" her mother asked from the bottom of the steps.

"Mom, I need you," she managed to say before sobs overtook her.

Her mother rushed up the stairs.

"Isidor's gone," Laura choked out.

"Oh, honey," her mother said, and took Laura in her arms. "I'm so sorry." She held Laura close and stroked her hair.

Laura's crying finally subsided, and she handed her mother the letter.

"Do you want me to read it?" her mother asked.

Laura nodded.

While her mother read the letter, Laura took some tissues from her night table and wiped her eyes and blew her nose.

Her mother gave the letter back to Laura. "It's so sad," she said. "But at least Paul's coming back. You must feel good about that."

"I do," Laura said. "And, Mom—I'm so glad you're here."

"Me, too, sweetheart. Why don't you come downstairs and keep me company while I start dinner?"

"Okay," Laura said. "I'll be down in a few minutes."

Her mother left, closing the door behind her. Laura picked up the letter and read it again.

She'd call Paul tonight. No, she'd write him. She needed time to think of the right words. Words for him, and for Miriam, too.

Standing up, she saw the late afternoon sun shining through her window. It wasn't getting dark so early anymore. In another month it would be spring. And in June, Paul would be back.

She opened her door and piano music drifted up to her. Charlie was playing something new, something incredibly sweet. Isidor never got to hear Charlie play. But Paul was coming back.

Paul was coming back.

Starting down the stairs, feeling drawn to the music, she wondered how it was possible to be so sad and so happy at the same time.

chapter twenty-eight

She saw him a block ahead, waiting for her at the corner of Magnolia Street. She waved to him and he waved back. The June air was sweet as she walked toward him.

"Hi," he said, and stretched out his hands.

"Hi," she said, taking his hands in hers.

For a moment, neither of them spoke. Then Paul pulled her to him. "Oh, Laura," he said, and then he was crying.

She felt a lump in her throat as she held him tight. And then she was crying, too.

"I'm sorry," he finally said. "I sure didn't expect that to happen."

"I know. I know. Me neither." She stepped back and looked at him, at his sad eyes. "I can't believe I'll never see your father again," she said. "Never hear him playing his music. Never hear his jokes. Never see his dear, sweet face. I guess you know I loved him."

"I know. And he loved you."

She reached into her pocket and found a tissue and wiped her eyes.

"Have you got one for me?" Paul asked.

"It's my last one, but I think it's still usable," she said, and offered it to him. "Want it?"

"From you? Sure." He took the tissue and wiped his wet cheeks.

Laura looked at him. He was tan. And taller.

"Hey, I think you've grown."

"Yeah. That's what Mom says."

"How is your mother?"

"She's okay. I have orders to bring you over. She wants to see you."

"I want to see her, too," Laura said.

"How's your mother?" Paul asked.

"She's good. Really good."

He took her hands.

"How does it feel to be back?" she asked.

"Great," he said. "Oops—I mean fantastic."

They both laughed.

She smiled at him. "So?" she said.

He smiled back. "So?" he said.